THE MONKEY'S MASK

DOROTHY PORTER has established a reputation as one of Australia's most exciting and innovative writers. Born in Sydney in 1954, she graduated from Sydney University in 1975, the same year as her first collection of poetry, *Little Hoodlum*, was published. Attaining a Diploma of Education, she supported her writing by part-time teaching for a number of years, before becoming a lecturer in Poetry and Writing at the University of Technology, Sydney. Her collection *Driving Too Fast* was shortlisted for the New South Wales Literary Awards in 1990. She currently lives in Melbourne. *The Monkey's Mask* is her eighth book, and her first for Hyland House.

Also by Dorothy Porter

Poetry
Little Hoodlum (Prism, 1975)
Bison (Prism, 1979)
The Night Parrot (Black Lightning Press, 1984)
Driving Too Fast (UQP, 1989)
Akhenaten (UQP, 1992)

Young Adult Fiction
Rookwood (UQP, 1991)
The Witch Number (UQP, 1993)

The Monkey's Mask

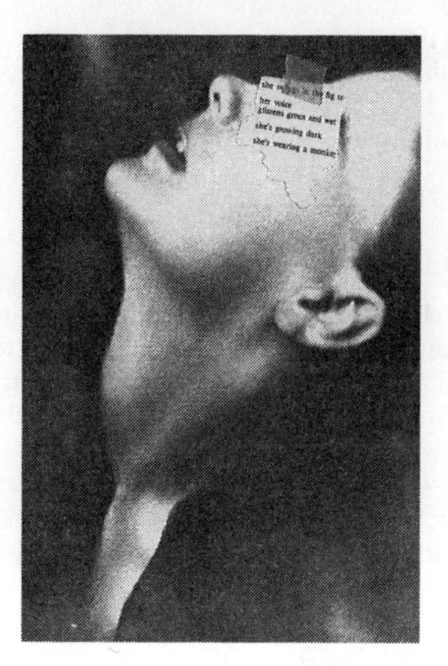

Dorothy Porter

HYLAND HOUSE

First published in 1994 by
Hyland House Publishing Pty Limited
Hyland House
387–389 Clarendon Street
South Melbourne
Victoria 3205

This book is a work of fiction. The characters, incidents, dialogue and plot are the products of the author's imagination or are used fictitiously. Any resemblance to actual persons or events is purely coincidental.

Publication of this title was assisted by the Commonwealth Government through the Australia Council, its arts funding and advisory body.

Australia Council for the Arts

National Library of Australia
Cataloguing-in-publication data

Porter, Dorothy Featherstone, 1954– .
The monkey's mask.

ISBN 1 875657 43 6.

I. Title.

A821.3

Cover and chapter headings designed by Vivienne Goodman
Typeset by Butler Graphics Pty Ltd, Richmond, Victoria
Printed in Australia by Australian Print Group

Chapters

Acknowledgements

My special thanks to the Literature Board of the Australia Council for its generosity in giving me the time and encouragement to write this book.

I would also like to thank my friends at Charles Sturt University for their support during my time as Writer-in-Residence.

The modest novelists, who helped me shape and edit the manuscript and made me appreciate the difficulties of narrative, deserve particular gratitude.

Excerpts from this novel have been previously published in *Southerly* ('Poetry' anthology issue), the *Bulletin* and the *Australian Book Review.*

Thanks also for permission to quote two lines from 'Money For Nothing' on page 151.

Year after year
On the monkey's face
A monkey's mask.

Basho

'What do you want a poet for?'
'To save the City, of course.'

Aristophanes

You see these grey hairs? Well, making whoopee with the intelligentsia was the way I earned them.

Dorothy Parker

for Gwen Harwood

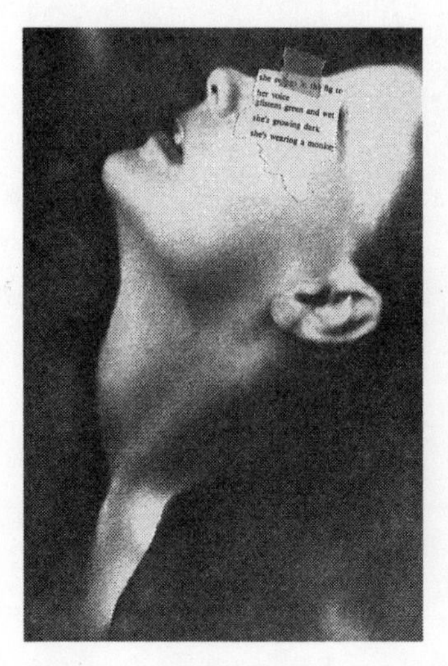
her voice
glistens green and wet
she's growing dark
she's wearing a

THE NEW JOB

Trouble

'Jill'
I challenge the mirror
'how much guts have you got?'

I like my courage
physical
I like my courage
with a dash of danger.

In between insurance jobs
I've been watching
rock climbers
like game little spiders
on my local cliff

I've got no head for heights
but plenty of stomach
for trouble

trouble
deep other-folks trouble
to spark my engine
and pay my mortgage

and private trouble
oh, pretty trouble

to tidal-wave my bed

I'm waiting

I want you, trouble,
on the rocks.

I'm female

I'm not tough,
  droll or stoical.

I droop
  after wine, sex
    or intense conversation.

The streets coil around me
  when they empty
I'm female
I get scared.

Blue Mountains recluse

I came for the quiet
I don't mind the cold

but thick mists
thick neighbours

and involuntary celibacy

are as inducive to hard drinking
as diesel fumes, high rent
and corrupt cops

I don't like bush walks
or Devonshire Teas

I can't remember what adrenalin
tastes like

I need Sydney
I need a new job.

My car

My place is my car.

Peace. Action.
Business and pleasure.

The glove box
crammed with tapes

Patsy Cline twining round me
like a clove cigarette

my windows my work
I spy with my little eye

the cheating world.

The new job

The phone's made of
foaming soap

I'm washing my hands

the phone's getting
smaller and smaller

but keeps ringing

ringing
it's the phone

christ, what's the time?
I wake up

too fast

the sun sharp
in the crack of the curtains

my feet freeze
as I pad to the phone

a woman's voice
pure North Shore

her phone manners
taking forever

yes, I'm Jill Fitzpatrick
yes, I do Missing Persons

how nice a friend of your husband's
remembers me

from a little internal matter
with his solicitor

cleared up nicely
client got his money back

father of six, Grand Mason Pooh-Bah
didn't go to gaol

yes, I remember
the hush money bonus

for a job discreetly done

and now the whole North Shore
loves me

so, Mrs Norris
you haven't seen your daughter

for how long?

Hungry

Money, I'm thinking money

as Mr Norris
in his blue faintly BO'ed suit
leans on the balcony rail
scaring the lorikeets off their sugar

a moody man
who signs the cheques
and lets his wife do the talking
when it's the kids not business

he hopes, as usual,
there's nothing money can't fix

I'm hopeful too

'There shouldn't be a problem'
I say to his tense shoulders
'I'll bring her home.'

Twinings

Insects float
black and frantic

on the smooth surface
of the swimming pool

Mrs Norris makes tea

Twinings
I bet myself

before it arrives
set out on a tray
a plump silver pot

my mother
would be proud of me

I sip Earl Grey
quietly

and let them talk
about Mickey

it's not like her
she doesn't take drugs
she doesn't even smoke

she wants to be a journalist

photos

she's pretty
she's sweet
she's too good to be true

her mother stands
brushes down her flowery frock

I take my cue
make reassuring plans

and glance
as I leave

the sun flattening
the withered rockery.

Someone's daughter

Mickey's father
    is a gent

and takes me to my car

'I'll be in touch soon'
I say
    holding out my hand

he takes it
    too hard and too quickly

a tremor
    in his squeezing fingers

I hold my breath
waiting for him to let go

'She isn't just pretty'
    the words sneaking
        through his teeth

'she's special'
I try to ease out
        my hand

he hangs on

'bloody special'

'I know, mate'
        I say gently

pulling my aching fingers
        free.

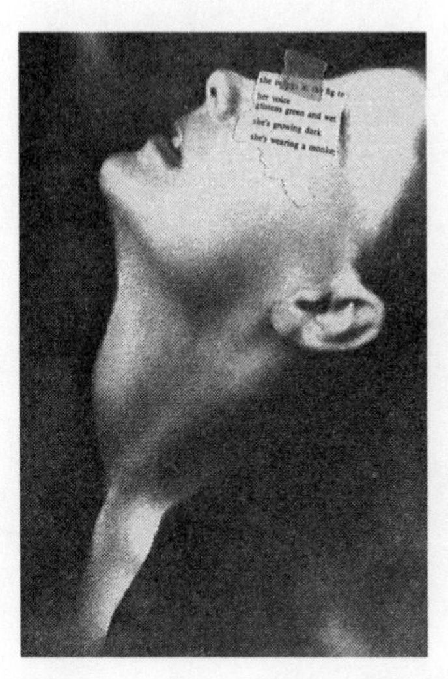

MICKEY'S FRIENDS

When the tears have dried

Mickey's bedroom
   in her parents' home
smells of floor polish
   and absence

'I'll have to tear
   this room apart'

I tell her mother
   who frowns
      at my gorilla hands

'What are you looking for?'
      she asks
'Drugs?'

'Anything'
I flip the mattress
'that tells me
   where she's gone
      and who with.'

She moans faintly
   and leaves me to it.

You have to be hard in this game.

I remember old Sid Lloyd's line –

'Never tell them
where their kid is
   until ya get paid.

When the tears have dried
no-one wants to part
   with money.'

Living in her head

I arrange to meet
Mickey's father
    on his own

doting Dads aren't always
    fools

'Does she like taking off
    on her own?'

he shakes his big sad head

'She's a very quiet girl,
    likes books'

he smiles

'she's like me
she likes
    living in her head.'

Uni cafeteria

In an aromatic stodge
of hot chips and meat
sizzle

students hold hands
blow smoke in each other's faces
and talk

was this Mickey's life
books, raving, drugs, gorging
and anorexia?

it was never mine
this sitting round with friends
and lighting up

nineteen I was in the force
primary school traffic cop
no danger

twenty-one still in the force
baby-sitting female juveniles
no gun

now thirty-eight
all muscle, street smart
no education

fun fun fun
I'm a mono Beach Boys record
my heart breaks

like surf.

Tianna

I spin the kid some bull
about being an old teacher
of Mickey's

I don't look like a teacher

the kid squints at me
suspiciously

'P.E.,' I say
and flex my muscles
under my shirt

she buys it

lots of fit-looking dykes
teach P.E.

but she's no fool
'Mickey hated sport.'

I laugh
like that's old news
'Couldn't do a forward roll
if her life depended on it!'

the kid
all black clothes
and black make up
what's her name?
– Tianna –

looks like glandular fever
and nicotine poisoning
on legs –

starts to relax
and offers me a cigarette

I hide the addict
in my eyes

'No thanks
put my training back a month.'

my voice hearty
as beef tea
across the smoke and laminex
student cafeteria

Tianna lights up anyway

'I haven't seen Mickey
since the Women's Reading'

I smile
with curiosity

she tells me all about it

she hasn't seen Mickey
for a fortnight

'There's a bug going round
Mickey said she felt a bit off.'

I get Mickey's address

it's the same one
her parents gave me

I try a shot in the dark

'Look'
all charm and *entre nous*
'I haven't seen Mickey
since she was at school
and I'm sure she doesn't tell
her folks everything,
is there a bloke in the picture?
I don't want to barge in
on something.'

the kid checks me out
I just pass

'Yeah, sure is'
she inhales
and takes the smoke
right to the bottom
of her lungs

'some fuckwit poet
Mickey reckons
is a big deal.'

I gasp like a groupie

'Who is he?'

she shrugs
'Mickey won't let on'

and pauses
to let in the Western Suburbs
with the tidbit

'he's married but.'

Flat-mates

You could skate on the grease
of the kitchen floor

a black puppy noses
the jammed-full bin

the girl yawns
the boy flicks ash on his crotch

still stoned.

'Look' I say
'I know it's early

I'm sorry
to get you up

I'm looking for Mickey

her parents are worried
just tell me where she is

and I can wrap this up.'

The girl yawns again
christ, it's not that early

my watch reads ten-thirty

'Late night, eh?'
I chuckle

I'm not much good
with the younger generation

she checks out my daggy jeans.

The boy's lips move under
blonde stubble

'No-one's under surveillance
in this house.'

he's got a student pollie's vocabulary
shot with a junkie's paranoia

I open a fresh packet of Drum

'Got any papers?' I ask
stupid question

in a room stinking
of stale dope

I roll three cigarettes

we smoke together
in the gungy air

I dig out two fifties
and smooth them flat

'One each
but I want some co-operation.'

the boy mutters 'bitch'
but pockets the money

'She's on the phone a lot'
the girl says

watching the boy

'to this arsehole
who makes her cry.'

'Does he have a name?'

the girl blinks

'Something common . . .'
she shrugs
'like "Fred".'

Mickey's room

Mickey's room
the only clean patch in the house

her bed-spread
patterned with blue moons

the floor
recently swept

her books
in alphabetical order

her shoes
lined up in the cupboard

her clothes
on hangers

her mirror
smear free

shows my face
pouch-eyed and wrinkled.

Not a lot of time for poetry

She slept on the floor
on a mattress

it looks comfy

By the pillows
in an upended packing case

an albino teddy bear
and two books

dust free

my knees crack
as I kneel to read them

poetry
Bill McDonald and Tony Knight

I've heard of McDonald

Jesus-Loves-Me shit
with the Snowy Mountains thrown in

the Saturday *Herald*
runs them sometimes

long fucking things

he must be set
on her Uni course

I flip through
the other book

smart arse stuff

only one poem
I can understand

about a teenage girl's
tits reflected

in a motel swimming pool

I read
thrillers myself.

Open books

Currawongs quarrelling
in the gum out my window

I'm going through a box
of Mickey's books

mainly poetry
mainly boys

McDonald and Knight
six volumes each

her favourites

I light a fag
dropping ash on an open page
of a McDonald masterpiece

flicking it clean
I read
Some girls are open books . . .

jesus, Bill, we must hang out
in different bars

Their breath as fresh on my face
as a brand new page . . .

Diana

The door reads
Dr Diana Maitland

I knock twice

she's thirtysomething
maybe forty

her hair honey-blonde
streaks

falls in her eyes
she pushes it back

with a fidgety
nail-bitten hand

she's got eyes
that flirt or fight

she's gritty
she's bright

oh christ help me
she's a bit of alright!

Tell me about you

'I can't talk here'
she says
'how about lunch?'

my grin's splitting me open

she grins back
like I'm fun not work

down in the lift
we chatter and spar

I'm breathlessly silly
we don't talk about Mickey

over lunch
I get rid of brass tacks quickly

'When did you last see Mickey?'

'Her poetry tutorial
a fortnight ago.'

'Did she mention
going away?'

Diana shakes her head.
'She was just her usual self.'

'What's that?'

'Intense and shy.
Like most poetry maniacs.'

Diana's finger dips
in the froth of my cappuccino

she licks her finger slowly

'Tell me about you'
she says.

Taste of a job

I like to taste
a new job

I like to follow
its flavour.

And this one?

Alcohol. A smooth red.

A taste
I'm not used to

a taste
going straight to my head.

Freak show

Am I Diana's freak show?

She wants to know all about it.
The bars. The scene.
All my old lovers.

'How many women have you slept with?'

I counted them up
    and told her.

Her clever eyes smirk
    and prise me apart.

We keep meeting for coffee
we don't talk about Mickey

could it be
she fancies me?

Spring

The spring trees
like Cracker Night sparklers

all over Sydney

every garden
every dead street
littered

under this flower fire

am I in love again?

my hands and heart
aching

for blossom
for wild wild risk.

The Happy Hour

It's House Riesling
and my third
in half an hour.

Christ, what's the time?

The Happy Hour
it says on the wall.

I'm happy all right
fucking hysterical.

Where is she?

One woman arrives
with her good legs

she could be her
but isn't.

Some other woman
has her pale freckled hand
curved around a glass

she could be her too
but isn't isn't.

Diana.

Her name climbs
from my toe-nails
to the bite of my teeth

and blooms
in my mouth
like a black-red rose

is it someone
wearing her perfume?

is it heart-burn?

is it the grog?

Little Aussie battler

'How can you stand
living so far
from the city?'
Diana asks
looking lovingly out
at Glebe Point Road

'My work isn't trendy'
I say
'it's mostly
in the Western Suburbs

I live in the Mountains
because Blacktown
or Penrith
would kill me.'

'My little Aussie battler'
Diana smiles
'my little Aussie snob.'

Mr Diana

'You're a pint-sized Cliff Hardy,'
Nick says
pouring me a beer

'Us real ones
come in all
shapes and sizes.'

Nick smiles.

He's pretty. pretty.
with his blonde pony tail
his soft blue jeans.

I can feel
Diana stroking him.

'Most of the PIs I get to meet
are big ugly pricks,
ex-cops
too bent
even for the force.'

'I'm an ex-cop.'
I tell
this young, leftie lawyer.

'Weren't you too short?'
Diana winks
and sips her gin and tonic

she's showing me up

her boy joins in

'How's your nose
for tracking down
North Shore brats?'

he picks his nose
    as he talks
too gorgeous to care

'Bit of a waste
  of a smart woman's time.'

'This smart woman
  needs the money.'

my voice gruff
  like a boy
    trying to hold his own
      with a man

Diana holds her glass up

'I knew you two
  would hit it off.'

Style

In love I've got no style

my heart is decked out
in bright pink tracksuit pants

it weaves its huge bummed way
through the tables to Diana

she's reading something
with very fine print

she doesn't need her glasses
to see me.

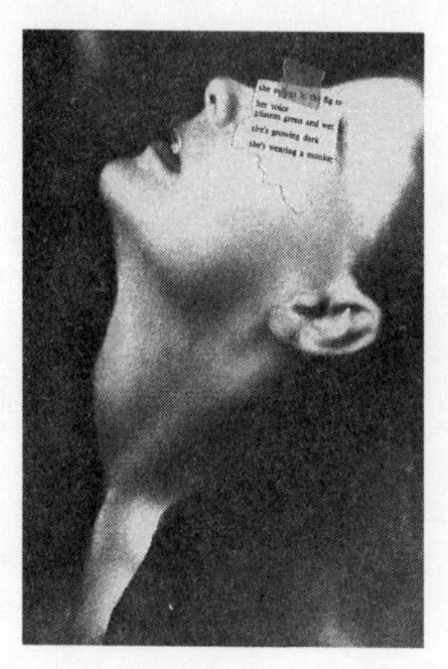

THE FULL MOON

Driving to her place

blue dusk

my car glides
        like a hovercraft

the wheel plays
        sweet
            in my hands

this time

will we just talk?

First move

I reach past my glass
  take her hand

I didn't plan this

my fingers freeze
on her warm veins

I can't read her eyes

silence

will she?
will she?

  touch me

I'm
right out in the open

I'm a fucking fool

oh jesus Diana

she's turning her hand
moist palm
    into mine

her skin

you could hear my heart
  in Perth

she picks up my hand
I swallow my tongue

she brings my hand
to her mouth

and sucks my ring
    finger

'you're trembling'
she says

my other hand
floats to her

touches her throat

her perfume
her eyes

the hot tip
of her tongue.

Wet

Here
I feel it here

flutter
groan
grind in the belly

what jellies my legs?
what flash-floods my cunt?

First time

we're laughing on her bed

my fingers struggle
   with her bra catch

'Didn't they teach you
this in Brownies?'

she lets her breasts free

they fall in my hands

her nipples grow
   between my lips

she strokes my hair
         'Jill'

my name in her mouth

my eyes close
in the musk and silk
         of her belly

her thighs
   under my nose

the sweetness of her

as she shudders
   on my mouth

'So that's what
   they taught you in Brownies'

she laughs in my arms.

The ex

'Why did you and Chris split up?'
  Diana asks.

'Listen, sweetheart,
I'll tell you
a dyke cautionary tale

about my one and only
marriage
my three-legged race

Chris and me
were as snuggly
as guinea pigs

our house our hutch
where it rained
carrots and lettuce

snuggly buggly
in our cuddly secret
we had a lovely life

until hand feeding
and bed-time stories
made us fat and dozy

and a big bad fox got in.'

'Oh dear'
  Diana says
    nuzzling my breast
'I promise
it won't be Beatrix Potter
    with me.'

'Good'
I sigh.

Legless

You forget

you get old and blunt

you forget what it's like

her taste on my mouth
her smell on my hands

the cops should pick me up
I can't walk a straight line.

Hanging around

I'm mooching around the phone

she said
she'd ring in a week

a week ago

is the fucking thing
out of order?

its dial tone drones
healthily in my ear

I'm giving myself the runs
from too much coffee

I'm smoking myself
sick

I've lost a kilo

I do aerobics
I practise karate

has the bitch
lost my number?

does Nick listen in
on all her calls?

the phone rings

I let it sing
for a delicious second

it's not her

Mickey's mother

she'll tie up the phone
for hours

the voice crumbles

'They've found her.'

Fuck all

I bet the little bugger
was up north
with her poet boyfriend
smoking dope
writing each other
sonnets

now she's back
for her pocket money

where does that
leave me?

with the retainer
and a few expenses

I did fuck all
apart from
fuck her teacher

the voice is whispering
the voice fades

'I can't believe she's dead.'

Bump

The wheel bumps
    over something soft.

A small tabby
    with a collar.

It twists
    in a broken somersault
        away from me

it's frothing blood.

Mickey's mother
I can't make her wait

a car stops behind me

please,
    I say,
      I'm in a terrible hurry

please,
    ring a vet.

A man
    with a furrowed burnt face
        and slow eyes

uh huh,
    he says
        looking down
            at the squirming cat

and I go.

Brandy

It's a beautiful night

a koel starts up
its one weird note

this time
we're drinking brandy
not tea

their faces slack
and grey

I talk to them
soothingly
they keep pouring brandy

I know the morgue
its stainless steel
its room freshener
and antiseptic smell

Mickey's father
cries first

her mother says

'We recognised her
by her clothes.'

In police hands

'It's now in the hands of the police'
Mickey's Mum's parting words
as I head for the door

hands of the police
hands of the police

it'd make you puke
to see anything
a can of coke, a smoke,
a Smith and Wesson
or a dead girl's skull
in Detective Sergeant Wesley's
thick fingers

I know his hands well

my last case
he took me in
showed me a cell
showed me the flat
of his hand

'No witnesses'
he said
wiping his palm
on the shine of his pants
'Whaddya call it, love?
Stop police attacks on women,
gays and blacks!
Let ya lezzo mates shout you a demo
for Christmas.'

two weeks later
he got decorated
for bravery

in police hands
Mickey in police hands

the night air sneaks
in my car window
yowling like an unfed cat.

Moonlight

The full moon
plops on a phone booth

in this freaky light
I could be standing

in a puddle of piss
I ring Diana anyway

'Mickey was murdered'

the words sound
stuttered and stupid

a shallow grave
in the National Park

I go on about dogs
digging her up

my hand shines white

'Doesn't this happen in your job
all the time?'

Diana's voice slaps me sober.

Then she makes
right noises

poor kid
how are her parents coping?

till she blurts
her news

'It's all happening!'

research grant come through
big offer from UCLA

I'm full of tired bullshit
I say

congratulations.

Brutal end for Mickey, petite, pretty and only nineteen

Mickey's murder on Page Three

under the big black headlines
the photo taken by her dad
at her eighteenth birthday party

'petite, pretty and only nineteen'
like a line from a sixties song

'sexually assaulted, strangled and dumped.'

Mickey in a police lens
chunks out of her arms and legs
from the pack of dogs that found her

barefoot,
    her shirt round her neck
    no pants,
her face swollen with rot

laid out by her killer
in the foetal position.

Dead kids

Dead kids upset me.

There's no drink
to take away the taste
of a fresh face rotting.

Useless
to tremble and vomit
and howl it's not fair.

You look at the spots
on the back of your hand
you look at the lines
fraying your face.

But you're still glad
it's the kid
not you.

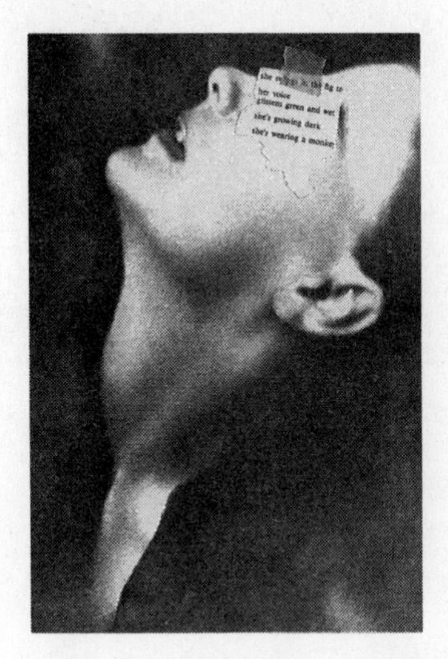

INSURANCE WORK

Mediterranean back

Three weeks of insurance work

binoculars, note-book, camera
and the car whiffy with chips

under observation
a squat Greek

top floor flat

he waddles out
into the street
with a brindled mongrel
that pisses on my wheel

is the Greek's wander
to the corner shop
a bit brisk
for a buggered back?

'Mediterranean back'
the boys at Mutual HQ
would say

did he hang that plant?

did he hit his mutt?

all very sus.

Oh christ.
Just write it up.

I'll ring you

And Diana.

Always this
  I'll ring you crap.

Sure, I say.

Sure
  because I don't want to hassle

sure
  because she's married

sure
  because something's better than nothing

  because her voice

  her breasts her mouth her smell

  make me stupid.

Family barbecues

Family barbecues
hit the nerve
like a drunk dentist

why didn't they reject me
when I came out?

I should be so lucky
to sit stiff-spined
and harmless
sipping warm beer
in the bedlam
of in-laws and kids

avoiding my mother's
  tolerant, anxious eye.

My mother

Why am I thinking
  about my mother?

my bum itchy
  on the hot seat

the dead quiet
  boring street

why am I thinking
  about my mother?

no music
just minding my own business

waiting for my crook-back Greek
    to do aerobics
        on his front balcony

I can't be conspicuous

  can't be conspicuous

Mum sniffs
    'Jill, you can look really nice
    when you want to

it won't kill you
  to wear a dress
    now and then.'

Mum touches my hair
'It used to be so pretty.'

and after three gin and tonics

'You don't have to be
    so conspicuous
we all know what you are.'

do you, Mum?
I'm curious. Fill me in.

What am I?

Shining footprints

My wet footprints
  shine
    on the floor

two phone calls in a row
  yank me
    out of the shower

my legs running water

second call
    Diana
and my breast perks
    out of the towel

'I don't care
  if every factory in Parramatta
  is torched tonight'

I don't pause for breath
    or pride

'Insurance Mutual can get fucked.
Mickey's mother has just rung
  she's jack of the cops
I'm back on the job.

oh, darlin', where ya been?'

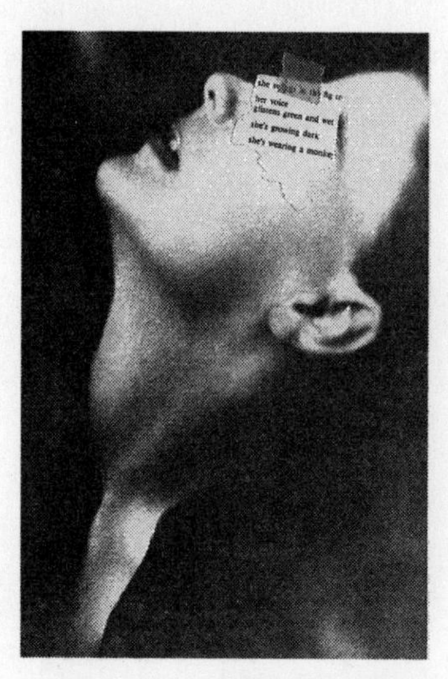

IN LOVE WITH AN INTELLECTUAL

Work

Today
I should be working

I should be going through
the coroner's report

asking questions

was Mickey killed
where her body was found?

what do the bruises
on her buttocks mean?

Today
I'm not working

I'm seeing Diana.

She buys me French champagne

'Veuve Clicquot'

I read the label silently
no French classes at my old school

my thumb strokes
   the cold green swelling
      of the bottle

'Don't swill it, sweetheart'
   she bubbles down my throat
'it's not Great Western.'

'I can read.'
   I watch her eyes
'What's the occasion?'

she takes a breath

I watch her hand
      in mid-air
before she pushes it
      through her hair

'I've missed you, Jillie.'

The best fuck

'Am I the best fuck you've ever had?'

Diana's chin on my thigh
  her eyes smoking up at me

I'm water turned to steam
  my skin scalded pink

I sigh
  wanting to gush
endearments, aching words, all my heart's
  stormwater banked up for weeks

Diana's cocky voice
  makes me bite my tongue

I hold out my arms

'No,' she says, 'I like to watch'

I give in
and feel her eyes touching me
  from throat to cunt.

Her clever hand

My car cassettes clatter
  at Diana's feet

'Don't you listen to boys?'

'I've spent my whole life
  listening to boys.'

I answer on feminist autopilot

she crosses her legs
she's wearing a dress

I drive and perve

her calves do a silky stretch
her hand taut with blue veins

as she slots in k.d.lang

'Butch country 'n' western'
she murmurs in the raunchy riffs

'Don't you ever forget I'm a dyke?'

she slips her clever hand
  between my thighs

to make me quiet.

Her breasts

Her breasts are not my breasts.

Under her dress
  they push
    towards my hands

Under my hands
  they push
    towards my breasts

they stop my heart.
they close my eyes.

she's not my mother
she's not my friend

    Diana. Dracula.

Her breasts suck me.

No thrillers

While she's in the toilet
I check out her books.

On the shelf
  thick books
  fresh-smelling paper
  academic stuff.

A muddle of novels
  by the bed
French and South American

no thrillers, no crap.

Does she bring her work home?

Or is this Diana?

Incessantly intellectual.

Street café

I hate street cafés

you're either
shivering in a gritty wind
or squinting
in the grimy sun

I fidget
Diana watches the traffic

'Here's Nick!'
she sits up

the coffee lumps in my gut

Nick swims over
nibbles her nose
and plops in a chair

'G'day' he says
'you're not too busy
dobbing in migrant Workers' Comp. cheats
to join two lefties for lunch?'

'Mate' I reply
'when I heard you were coming

it was a simple case
of pleasure before business.'

he laughs
'You're a brazen little tart.

What are ya having?
It's on me.'

Dyke Othello

'You know' Diana says
   her mouth moving on my
      collar bone
'I only love you for your stories.
      You're my dyke Othello.'

I don't know
what she's on about

but it sounds like
a compliment

I chew on her ear
'Have I told you about the time
I worked for Jacquie Biquette?'

'No!'

Jacquie's such a big deal
   in the jazz and short black set

'Well, she's a dyke'

'Christ, is she?
Doesn't look like one.'

I let that pass.

'She hired me in the strictest
confidence'

I'm blabbing

'to check up on her girlfriend
a baby dyke
into older women and expensive leathers

when she's not bludging off
   some poor besotted bitch

she's making home grown videos
for Canberra's mail order
porn market.

Jacquie was just plain old-fashioned
jealous

she thought she was seeing
another woman

I had to trail that little slag
through every girl bar

from here to Melbourne.'

Diana pinches one of my smokes

'And was she?'

'Not another woman.
Just women.
All shapes and sizes.
From ex-Mulawa koories
to Toorak lipstick dykes.'

Diana grins
'That's a good story.'

she'll tell Nick

why can't I keep my mouth shut?

The old bag

Her cheek soft and sticky
on my breast

I stroke out the knots
  in her hair

'You're going grey
  over your ears'

my voice
  soft and sticky

'I'm just an old bag'

her breath making
  my nipple hard

'Is that what Nick calls you?'

have I gone mad?

she doesn't move
nothing but her breath
and the ache in my tit

I close my eyes
and wait for her
to leave

'Nick doesn't notice
the grey over my ears'

she kisses my breast

'Nick doesn't notice
anything.'

My sweetheart

'My shout'

in my hurry
my wallet spills its guts
all over the floor

Diana picks up my plastic
fastidiously

then pounces
on a photo

'I thought I was
your sweetheart'
she says

tracing the line
of Mickey's jaw
and neck

with a chewed nail.

Discretion

'Does Nick know about us?'

I'm not tasting
    my croissant

she helps herself
  to my rollies

and keeps me waiting

'Why would you mind
    if he did?'

'Because'
my voice
    tight as asthma
'he's a perve
because
it's our business'

Diana smiles

'He likes you
he likes
    talking about you
almost as much

as I do.'

Louie

Louie's a New Ageing
lesbian poet
an old mate

and my guide to the poetry scene

over a rabbit food lunch
I talk about nothing
but Diana

Louie crunches her carrot

'What's her star sign?'

'I don't know
next time I see her
I'll ask for you.'

'She must be a Cancer'
Louie picks the walnuts
out of her salad
with nicotine-stained
fingers

'Diana is a Moon name
a witch name'

Lou's eyes
half glitter at me
and half perve
at the young blonde butch
sniggering
with her girlfriend
at the next table

'all Moon women are Cancers.'

'Well,' I confess
'my Diana sure waxes
and wanes.'

Louie frowns

'Tell me more
    about the murdered girl

tell me
    what you're doing.'

Good legs

I'd kill for good legs.

Mickey had legs
that would have stopped
traffic –

traffic. traffic.

my mind's jammed.

Is it easier
lusting after Mickey's legs
  than looking at her face?

Through the static

My mobile phone pings
it's Mickey's father

I drive with one hand
as he stammers through the static

'When you know
who killed her

don't tell the police
tell me

I'm not going to wait
for his light sentence

I'm not going to wait
for his parole

let the social workers wail
about his terrible childhood

after I've finished with him.'

I try to reassure him
until I hear a noise

it's not crying

it's worse.

No chips

At this book launch
you pay for your drinks
at the bar

and listen to the writer
and her best friend
and her editor

make long speeches

my stomach growls

'Lou, where's the chips?'

Illiterate and stupid

Is it me?

Is it because I left school
at sixteen?

I don't understand
this crowd.

I've lost Lou

she's busy
working the room

'schmoozing'
she calls it
giving me a wet kiss
ordering me
to have another drink
and hang in there

she's found him
Mr Poetry Business
a wanker with a pubic bush
red beard
and a big voice
that spits

I've-got-a-big-dick
epics
all over the front row

Lou says
he could help us

what about
the academic feminist

with her long poem
about a Greek goddess
doing the dishes

can she help us too?

Or is it just me?

Illiterate and stupid.

Just like the brain-dead cops
  Nick loves
    demolishing in the witness box.

Barbara

Louie's nose ring
  distracts me

as she jerks her face
  into my cheek
    whispering
'That's Barbara!
Tony Knight's wife.'

Tony Knight!
'I found his books
all autographed affectionately
in Mickey's room . . .'

'They had the whole scene
    sewn up'
      Lou goes on
'before Tony pissed off
    to Brisbane.'

her lips moving on my cheek,
  bloody incorrigible.

'You couldn't fart
   in the poetry scene
   without Barbara's permission,
Tony's two cents worth
   in the *Herald*

could mean a grant
    or a publisher.'

I nod
  watching Barbara light
    a cigarette
with tiny pretty paws

Louie's breath tickling
moist

'You know why Tony's in Brisbane?
Barbie's after his balls'

Barbara's eyes
even across a smoke-filled room
      are beautiful
            and beautifully made up

'Tony runs a casting couch
      for young female poets,
Barbie caught him
   giving some sweet hopeful . . .'

I straighten my shoulders
forcing Lou back

and see Mickey's nervous fingers
  spreading out in Tony's lap
    pages and pages of poems.

Kicking corns

At another launch
    generously catered
I jump
  in front of Barbara Knight

'Yes?'
  her voice tense and pleasant
    with all those private school vowels

where do I know you from?
  her eyes click over me
    like computer keys

I put her out of her misery.

'I'm a private investigator'

and tell her my name

'Wondered where you fitted in'
  she murmurs
    with her party smile

'I'm on the Mickey Norris case'
  I test the water

she lifts a drink
    from a passing tray
without spilling a drop

'That's a trick
    you must teach me'
I'm twinkling

Barbara takes in
  my finger-combed butch hair
and stops herself flirting
  cold

'Mickey who?'

'Norris.
A young fan of your husband's.'

'Well?'

Doesn't Barbara read the paper?

'She went missing . . .'

'Missing what?'

'Taste?'
  I suggest

she turns on her neat heel

leaving me
holding my end of the repartee
    like an empty glass.

Poetry Reading

Gut rot grog

Diana warned me
about poetry readings

'They're only supposed to read
for fifteen minutes,
you'll learn
Einstein's Theory of Relativity
first hand, my dear,
fifteen minutes can stretch
like an old rubber band.'

Can Bill McDonald read a watch?

He's been up there
for at least an hour
no. only ten minutes.

Jesus.

I'm starting to hallucinate.

No wonder
Diana wouldn't come.

I've tried listening.

Bill calls light 'dusky'
in every bloody poem

and he's got a thing
about his grandfather's hat

the lucky old bastard
must be dead.

Come on, Bill,
that's it, mate,
last fucking poem

I'll be dead and burnt to ashes
before Bill's dusky light
    sets
        on his Grandad's hat.

Hippy poets

After the break
it's a hippy circus

three pretty boys, one mug girl,
tossing their curls

shouting their poems
between costume changes

whales and rainforests
line after blubbering line

get me a harpoon
get me a bulldozer

better still
fetch my wicked woman

darling, don't make me sit
through this shit

on my own.

How do you talk to poets?

We shake hands
and I'm stuck

how do you talk to poets?

I'm not known for my love
of fluffy clouds
fields of daffodils
or brumbies on a moonlit night

give me a good bottle of wine
a woman with spit and spark
and the Trifecta at Randwick

'You're a sensitive man,
Mr McDonald, and I'd like to discuss
a sensitive matter.'

He smiles.

He's tall, pale and limp
like the kind of pasta
that dribbles on your shirt
on a first date

his mouth is arrogant
and nervous

he licks his thin lips
with a whitish tongue

'How can I help you?'

the sort of voice that wows
the First Year Arts girlies
all ears in the front row

'I'm investigating the murder
of Mickey Norris.'

'Are you a police officer?'

His eyes patronise
the girl constable.

'No. I'm working for Mickey's parents.'

'That poor girl.
A shocking thing.'

'Did you know her?'

'She wrote to me
and sent her poems,
an occupational hazard
for a poet on the H.S.C.'

'The price of fame, mate'
I say without thinking

he snags on my gag

'I don't suppose you get much fan mail
in your line of work.'

he plays with the cross
around his neck
oh christ, a Christian

'Did you ever meet Mickey?'

'No. Just a correspondence.'
clutching his cross

'What did she write about?'

'Nothing much.
I told her I was busy.'

'She was the keen one
in this correspondence?'

'She wanted me
  to look at her poems.'

'And did you?'

'Yes.
One or two.'

He looks over my shoulder
  and wiggles his eyebrows
    at a pal

'Look, this is a terrible business
but that's all the help
I can give.'

'Can I see the poems
she sent you?'

'I'm sorry.
I tore them up.'

he tucks away his cross
and shuffles his feet

'Why?'

He frowns.
'They were obscene.'

he smiles as thinly
as packet soup
and slips away.

Kept girl

'How much did you pay
for those sunglasses?'

'Eight dollars ninety-five'
I say
'keep your eyes on the road'

she overtakes
on the inside
a family man in a Volvo

I love watching her drive
I love watching her
take risks

I put my hand on her knee
she's warm through her
stocking

'I'll buy you a new pair'
she says
stroking my hand

'Pair of what?'
my mind turns to
black lingerie

she kisses my fingers

'Sunglasses.'

If you don't know me by now

Diana's tongue whirls
    in my mouth

like a dissolving aspro
like knives on a chariot wheel in *Ben Hur*

twisting her hair in my hands
I bring her in so close
her teeth grate on my teeth

this close
she's hard not soft

this close
she's teeth not tongue

this close
she's hurting me.

Poem on the answering machine

I hit my front door

a clammy mist
   coiling around my feet

like a Transylvanian
   welcome mat

my house smells
   of an empty long day

as I turn on
   the answering machine

a precise male voice fills the room

'Fitzpatrick, you stupid cunt
you're playing with your life
so don't take a punt

I know where to find you
I'm just taking my time
before I do what I do

you don't know me
but, slut, I know you
just wait and fucking see

so now I'll end my pretty poem
I hope you've got the message –
expect a visit when you're home.'

I light a fag

and play my telephone poem
   over and over.

Nostalgia

'I'm always here if you need me'
Chris knows me too well

I grab at the old love in her voice
it's a double brandy

oh, Chris, I feel like blubbering,
I'm nearly forty
I'm in love again
I'm tracking a strangler
I'm reading poetry
I'm getting so sensitive
I'm an allergy on legs

instead
we talk about women's self-defence
classes
and with good will on both sides
Chris's partner's new job
karate instructing

'Maybe I should employ her'
I joke
'I could do with some muscle'

Chris can pick up
my tremors from Mars
'Are you all right?'

oh, she's always been my lamb's wool
my lulling lake

if she were here
I'd throw myself against her soft breasts
and
be in the same suffocating mess
all over again

no
  I made my choice two years ago
the cold air, the lovely leg stretch
  of the single life

we sign off
  with the matey crackle
    of old lovers
      and unsteady friends

I put down the phone
  rub my eyes and sigh

nostalgia balloons
  in my chest

until Diana rushes back
like an IV'ed amphetamine.

Diana's poems

'Do you write poetry?'

it's an after-great-sex question
my nose
    in Diana's armpit
her heart still fast
    under her light sweat

her answer
    breathless

'Sometimes
  but
    not for publication'

I luxuriate
  in the fantasy
    of Diana's poems
put my face
    eyes shut
in the steam of them

'Could I read some?'

she slowly shifts
    away

my nose lies
  on the sheet

'What for?
they're not about us

they're not about
    anything.'

State of the art

'The Smack Discourse in Jazz'
Diana says
shaking out the last cigarette
  from her pack of Benson and Hedges

'what a great title for a thesis!'

Billie sings the blues
  on the CD player

her stoned musky voice
  hiccups in my cunt

Diana is talking too much
she's so fucking clever
I just want to go to bed

Nick's in Melbourne
we've got all night

Billie's drifting away
Billie's sticking it all up her arm

I'm seeing double

'She's making me depressed'
my words slow and slurred

Diana's eyes gleam
watching that exquisite noise
    machine

'Nick picked it up in Tokyo'
    she says

'it's state of the art.'

Love me a little

I want to say

it's no good
when I'm in this mood

abused children are crawling
through my hair

wives with hammer-shattered heads
are smeared on my eyeball walls

Mickey's skull whistles
through its black holes

I've got the male violence DTs

while Diana lies in my arms
working me over
with her hands

I want to say

I can't come
let's talk instead
oh, christ, love me a little

but it's no good

it's Diana
it's a drink that takes me right
    over the edge.

My throat

'Your throat'
she says

licking
along my neck

'gorgeous'

her throat
thrums
against my breast

I'm stunned

her finger runs
down
my wind-pipe

I gulp

'your throat'
she says

'is state of the art.'

What it's like

Mickey was strangled.

Enough of her left
to establish that.

Diana put her hands
around my throat

'Wanta see what it was like?'

pressing the balls of her thumbs
in

her lips grazing my eyes
her knee in my cunt

jerking between suffocation
and coming

I can't remember if it was nice
or not.

What she is

Driving home
the dawn full moon

pulling me up
the Mountains

my heart slops about
in my chest

the moon knocks
on the windscreen

just love her
the moon says

stop checking your change
no one's ripped you off

just love her
love her

for what she is.

Word for today

'Word for today'
hisses the voice on my answering machine

'is love.'

a breathy pause
like the voice is counting to ten

'Love
has the same number of syllables as
dead'

the word comes for me
full of stiletto spit

'our word for tomorrow.'

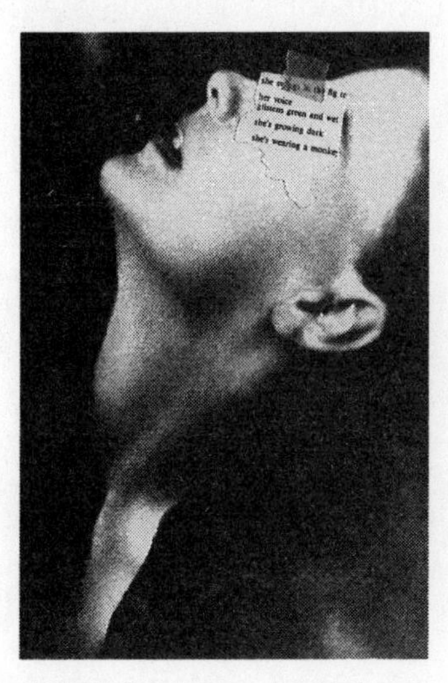

MICKEY'S POEMS

Victim poetry

Mickey's poems.

Some written for Diana's class
others I'd found hidden
    in her room.

Diana spreads out a sample
    over dinner

she'd marked them hard.

All I read
    is a whimpering voice.

Who were they for?
Who kicked her around?

Diana shrugs
    and picks at her chicken

'Victim poetry —
my female students love it.

Why do you think
  I prefer teaching fiction?'

I smooth out a page.

Your eyes, your eyes
I glance
Bullets and knives.

Bullets and knives

Your smell fills the room like flowers
but your eyes fill my heart like thorns
you care about the pain of the poor
why can't you feel my pain?
would you hold me gently if I was Aboriginal?
would you listen to my dreams
if I spoke battered English?
hold me, listen to me
forget who I am, forget I'm pretty
pretend I'm disadvantaged
because around you I don't have to pretend
I'm disadvantaged
you make me unemployed
you make me persecuted
you make me black
you make me very blue
help me like you help others
even your cum smells like flowers.
Your eyes, your eyes
Bullets and knives.

'Poor little petal'
Diana sighs

'falling for Christian crap.'

she flicks at the page
and laughs

'stupid little fool

mistaking born-again Bill
for St Francis.'

Your heart of ferns

Let me put my face in the creek
that runs through your heart of ferns
all your beautiful words run in the water
like beautiful fish kissing my mouth
let me stroke the big green fronds
that grow huge like wet spears in your heart of ferns
and I will sing like a bird that knows its God
because I know you like no-one else ever will
you've handed me a green key that I will always love
because I've seen your holy beautiful face
because I've kissed your beautiful feet like Mary
because you're a man with a spirit like pure gold
because you're my beautiful secret that I can carry
like a fire into your heart of ferns
where I'll burn you up
where I'll melt your lips on mine
where I'll rub your ashes into my skin
holy man, your heart of ferns is not safe with me
you'll smell me coming with my box of matches.

'I quite like this one.'

Diana watches the froth
  of my cappuccino
    spill into my saucer.

'You must be pre-menstrual' she says.

My beautiful man

I can't talk to you, my beautiful lover
I can't talk to you, my beautiful man
I can't talk to you, I can't talk to you
you listen with your cock in my mouth
you listen with your knee on my throat
you listen with your beard voice
scratching me out
you tell me I've got nothing to say
I'm just a cunt
your cock has all the words
you pump them into me
till I can't stand up
till I'm nothing
till I'm just dripping you
everywhere, everywhere
beautiful lover, beautiful man, let my poem do my talking
let it stand up and whisper in your heart
I love you I love you I'll love you till I die
even if your angry cock kills me.

'Jesus!' I whistle
'This poem needs tongs!

sweetheart,
  what were you setting those kids
    for homework?'

Your floating hair

Your hair is a storm that breaks over my face
Your hair is lightning and hail stones on my lips
Your hair tickles down my throat like a peacock feather
I want to drown in your beautiful hair
I want to stuff it in my pillow case
I want to die in it and wear it as my shroud
Float Float Float away on your beautiful hair
and go to Heaven.

'This couldn't be Bill McDonald'
      I help myself to Diana's fags
'he's going bald.'

'Infatuation is blind,' Diana says
'and anyway she nicked the floating hair
        from Coleridge.'

I watch my smoke floating
        over her messy curls.

As it really is

I know the world as it really is.
Endless war, my heart in flames.
But I can smell the sweetest water
When I swim in that water
I am an Angel.

so, Mickey, you reckon
you knew the world

someone knew you

someone who likes
tearing the fins off angels.

Fish out of water

Bill's in his element

a lunchtime reading
for the blue rinse set
and schoolkid conscripts

Lou isn't

'Everyone's staring at me'
she squirms

'You owe me'
she adds

Bill's at the podium
talking
at humorous length

his schooldays in the bush
God

and gee whiz it's great
to be an Australian

the crowd is hushed

it's Bill's day

get under his skin
get him with his guard
down

I wait for interval
and grab Lou

'I'll stand behind you.
Gush.'

'Wrong girl, Jill.
He hates dykes.'

‘Move’
I knee her in the bum

Bill’s face
so aquiline
so modestly sensitive

changes and chills
when he see Lou

‘I grew up in the bush too’
she lies

the tyre over the swimming hole
Grandma’s wallaby tail soup

just getting into her stride
when Bill spies me

and throws my timing
right off

‘Excuse me’
he says to Lou

moving into a claque
of middle-aged fans

I go for his sleeve
and miss

‘I’ve found her poems’
I hiss

‘all of them!’

suddenly I feel
a heavy hand
tightening on my arm

it's a huge woman
in a purple dress

'Dear' she says
'don't push.'

Bill grins gratefully
and disappears
   into his element.

Sentimental

At my STD expense
Diana and I have
one of those long phone calls

that leave you famished

she ignores my tired flirting
and brings up Mickey

'For sheer sexual rapacity
even you, Jill, couldn't keep
up with that kid

she must have screwed
every poet in Sydney'

she laughs
'excluding the girls.'

my armpits itch
my heart howls

'She was looking for something'
I mumble

'maybe something for her poetry
in those arseholes.'

Diana's breath stings
down the line

'You ex-Catholics are so sentimental
next you'll be making
a little plaster statue

and calling it The Virgin Mickey.'

Wrong number

The phone rings

I turn on the light
  ungum my eyes
  clear my throat

'Jill Fitzpatrick'
I unravel my sleeping name

the phone clicks

I wake up cold shower
  fast

it's four o'clock

it's pitch outside

I wait

I know this game

the phone rings

I wait

let it ring

I pick it up

listen

the phone clicks

I put it down
  reach for my pistol

take off the safety catch

a floor board creaks

I light a cigarette

the phone rings

I'm fast

you've got the wrong number, fucker

the phone sits tight

I sit with it

chainsmoking

cradling my gun.

Phone calls

The phone

my hand's shaking
I should stick to insurance work
  and paid perving

it's Chris
in a long distance voice
'Mum died on Saturday
we cremated her this morning.'

one of those slow cancers
bowel or stomach
not in a hurry
like brain or lung

wastes you down to nothing

I've been getting phone calls

a dirty handkerchief voice
chatting about another death

mine

it may be slow
it may be lingering

no blubbering this time
on Chris's shoulder

I turn on the tellie
and watch the body count
from a shopping mall massacre

there's imagination in that voice

like Mickey
I'm marked for something special.

If love was just talking

What are you saying to me?
What is it I can do to ease your pain?
I'm young but I'm not insensitive
I don't need coffee to stay awake all night
thinking about you and what I can do
because love isn't just talking
because my love isn't just words
do you want it in italics?
do you want it in bold print?
do you want it on fax?
do you want it on your mobile phone?
I'm here for you
I'm not just a hole for your prick
I can feel your pain even when you come
even though every groan, every sigh you make
is magic to me.

Diana pushes the page towards me
'Definitely
  to a suffering boy poet.'

'Bill or Tony Knight?'

'Bill. He'd lap it up.'

'But he's a Man of God and'
  I shudder
'so repulsive.'

'Sure. To a godless dyke.'
    Diana smiles her crooked smile
'Not to the sensitive eye
  of a budding
    and ambitious poetess.'

'Would Bill have a mobile phone?'

'C'mon, darling.
  It's called poetic licence.'

Skin-deep

I love the lines
  around her eyes

I love the faint folds
  of soft skin on her throat

her furrowed brow
  over Mickey's poems

makes me lick my lips

and I can't hear a word
    she's saying.

The pong poem

'Well' I say
watching Lou's face
still for once
while she reads
a sample of Mickey's poems

'Bill or Tony?'

Lou's huge eyes glisten
as she stares through me

she's not about to cry?

'Jill'
her voice is shaking
'this isn't a joke'

she's not upset
she's furious

'I don't want
to even think
about you and that bitch
sniggering over this kid's
hurt

this kid's
humiliation'

'Leave Diana out of this.'

'Why can't you?'

'Lou, help me
you know the scene'

and I push
Bullets and knives
up her nose

'who's the fucker
    in this poem?'

Lou biffs it
    away
and glares into space

'You're looking for a poet
    who pongs
        like a bathroom freshener

and I can't think of one.'

What you taught me

I wait for you not with a trembling heart
but with a trembling mind
you walk in and the room hushes
like you were a mysterious goddess
and while you talk I tremble
your words go through me like lasers
I can't keep up with you
I don't want to
I don't even want to be you
I just want to learn
I just want to listen
and drink drink you in
you're a mystery
you've taught me to love mystery.

'Lou, this one's
   up your alley.
   Help me track down
      a goddess.'

'Christ, you're stupid'
      she snarls
'did you show it
      to your girlfriend?'

'Diana's read them all.'

'And what did she say
   about this little beauty?'

'She said it's a red herring.
We're looking for a boy.'

'Was this in the pile of poems
   she showed you?'

'No.
   It was among the lot
      in Mickey's room.'

'Who do you think it's to?'

'I haven't a bloody clue.'

'Let me help you.
It's Mickey's version
   of *To Sir With Love.*
It's breathless gratitude
   to her fucking teacher.'

Lou slurps her tea
   and smiles

'Reads more like
   breathless infatuation'
      I say
         wanting it to go away

'I suggest'
   Lou's pompous
      in her triumph
'you workshop this one
   with your girlfriend
      again

you must be a slower learner
   than Mickey.'

Apples for teacher

I watch Diana
  shredding her serviette
    as she talks

and imagine
  those lovely hands
    talking in the air

'Are all your students
    besotted with you?'

'To most of them'
    she snorts
'I'm just a boring old bag.'

'Poetry classes must get
  pretty intense'

I feel my way

'do any of them
  ever write poems
    to you?'

'There's always a romantic
    cretin
        or a crawler.'

her hands are still
her voice is steady

'Did Mickey write you a poem?'

'If she did
  she kept it to herself.
She liked boys.
  Boy poets.

Sweetheart, for Mickey
  other women
    were competition
      not inspiration.'

I laugh
    and agree.

Goodbye Mrs Chips

'Why are you helping me?'

she looks up
  and rubs her eyes

'Because I can't afford
to have any more
of my poetry class
  bumped off.'

she barely smiles
she sounds exhausted

'You must have cared
for Mickey'
I say

reaching across
to touch her

'Just call me "Mrs Chips".'
Diana picks up
  Mickey's poem

ignoring my hand.

Torture

Love is a torture.
Love tortures me.
Does Love torture you?
If it does why are you laughing?
I feel you in the room like a knife.
You'll cut out my heart.
You cut out my cunt.
So why not cut out my heart?
Your prick is a knife that hurts me.
You grunt like a beautiful pig.
I wish my cunt could hurt you.

'Some bastard
  was giving her a very hard time.'

Diana yawns
  and touches my cheek

'Oh, Jillie,
  you're so sweet.'

The death smell

'Why were Mickey's poems
so violent?'

Diana stretches
  her warm arm
    over my face

'Dunno.'

her perfumed skin
doesn't make me dopey

I want to crash through

'Her poems
are so desperate
it's hard thinking that kid's
dead.'

'We've all got to go
sometime, darling.'

her tongue wet
on the inside of my wrist

so easy
to go under

'Have you ever seen a corpse
before the funeral parlour
tarts it up?

I'll never forget the zip
of my first body bag

there's the smell –

disinfectant and old piss
and something else
that crawls in your stomach
later

the death smell

it stays on you
for days.'

she's chewing her fingernail

'You don't give a flying fuck, do you?'

'Stop shouting at me' she says

'Go home
to your pretty man
he doesn't give a stuff

you might as well live
with a state-of-the-fucking-art
fridge.'

her eyes are cool

'Weren't you a big brave girl
to sniff a stiff.'

For Diana

I'll write you a poem, bitch

get me a pen
get me some paper

I'll scratch your name
in green ink

the sizzle of lust
the colour of poison

I'm not at your feet
I'm at your throat

your drugged dope
your moray eel

knows your lowest moan
knows you better

than who gets to pet you
at home

I'll write you a poem, bitch

get me a pen
get me some paper.

Mickey

What was it like
  to be you?

Louie believes in ghosts.
I don't.

I'm talking to your photo.
I'm talking to myself.

What was it like
  to be you?

I never had the legs
for your tight black skirts

I never got the hots
for fucked-up older men.

You with your shiny hair
and big smile for doting Dad

we're so different, kid.

Where the girls are

'I knew it'
  Diana's hand
    suddenly
      strokes up my skull
'you're a prude.'

her eyes are wonderful
    in the dinge

I sip my watered-down white
  and feel my pants
      get wet

'Just look at her now'
    Diana's voice moist
        on the lobe of my ear

on stage
  a purple-mouthed blonde
    in crotchless leathers
      angling her cunt
        over a prone brunette's face

I couldn't care less

'Oh, look at her nipple rings'
    Diana tongues my ear

I want to go straight back
    to her place

my fingers crunch her fingers
'Spectator sport bores me.'

'Nick's seen this show.
They're just warming up.
Wait.
  You won't get bored.'

'What?
  not bondage and discipline?'

'Wait.'
    Diana licks her lips.
'Just wait.'

How can I tell

How can I tell
she doesn't love me?

easy

it's not just her fidgeting fingers
  or how often
    she doesn't touch me

it's the slack of her shoulders
it's the slack of our talk

I'm too easy

she doesn't love me.

Secrets

'Why do you stay with Nick?'

why do I poke and pry
   after meltdown sex?

the window rattles
as a truck goes by

I dig into her eyes

'Smile' she plays
   with the corners of my mouth

I don't let up

'All right' she sighs

'because
   he shares his secrets

because
   he lets me in.'

Terrific day

'You're a great fuck'
   Diana says from nowhere

driving
   with one hand

her other
   playing in my lap

this is turning out
   a terrific day

'but'
   she adds

'you're a very ordinary
   detective'

she always
   poisons everything

enjoying herself
   behind her shades

'no wonder you're broke, Jill.'

I look down at her hand

'Drop me off'
   I say quietly

'next set of lights
   drop me off.'

Drinking you off my mind

The bottom of my glass
    reflects worse news
than just the red eyes
    of your 'ordinary detective'

there's that blurred blobby look
    of the loser

do I blame lust
  or my laziness?

I wish I could blame you.

Filthy language

'We didn't bring her up
  to use words like that.'

Mickey's mother puts the folder
on the side table

'Is that what they call poetry
    these days?'

she wipes her hands together
    delicately

'Is that what they were
    teaching her
        at that place?'

'No' I say
  'her poetry tutor thinks it's – '

(*crap*
  Diana's face droll and cruel
    over a short black)

' – not really up to scratch.'

Mickey's mother stares into
  some bleak beautifully furnished
    middle distance

'She didn't use that sort of language
    at home.'

I'm on my third cup of weak tea

is she crying
because her daughter
  wrote cunt in a poem?

'They're love poems,'
  I say

the dust motes go crazy
  in her expelled breath

she mops up her eyes
    furiously

'Then she must have been a monster!'

her flat chest
  rises and falls
    under her nice frock.

Sex and poetry

I never knew poetry
   was about
opening your legs
   one minute

opening your grave
   the next

I never knew poetry
   could be
as sticky as sex.

Dancing

'I can't dance.'

'I'll teach you'
Diana says
already moving
as she pulls me
to my feet

strobe light
cuts the smokey room
into pieces
of sizzling white

a silver-breasted boy
rippling on his fast feet
dances on his own

'Isn't he gorgeous . . .'

'Sure is' Diana smiles
'it's Nick.'

Isn't he sweet? Isn't he gorgeous? Isn't he mine?

Nick's been out all night
but smells fresh

he sips his short black
and piles in the sugar

'Aren't you sweet enough,
mate?'

he winks back
we both like this game

'Wanta cup?'
he says

'There's no rush.
Diana's doing her face

and Rome wasn't built
in a day.'

His eyes sparkle
his hands opening the paper

to read about himself
are soft

neither of us hear
Diana creeping in

I smell her perfume
and turn around

'My two crusaders'
she says

her voice is soft
her eyes sparkle.

Water and chemicals

Is it a wall
or a pit
or a poked wound
that grows between lovers?

I've been reading too much poetry

perhaps it's much simpler

just shake up two skin jars
of water and chemicals

bump them hard
together

and watch their chains
of strange molecules
change and groan.

Advice

'Don't flush your life
down the toilet . . .'

STD still pipping

'Lou'

'I haven't finished.
You know I'm psychic'

'Not now'

'Shut up.
That woman's trouble.
I'm telling you
big bloody trouble.'

'I'm a big girl'

'What about Mickey?
What are you doing?
She's keeping me awake.
She's haunting me, Jill.'

'Cut the Twilight Zone crap.'

Lou takes a breathy drag
and makes me want
just one more fag

'She was raped and strangled
and buried like shit.
Your mind should be on murder, Jill,
not your cunt.'

I'm too tired to get mad

'I'm doing my best . . .'

'To get into that bitch's pants.'

'Go write a dirty poem, Lou.'

How poems start

Is this how poems start?

when every riff on the radio
hooks in your throat

is this how poems start?

when the vein under her skin
hooks in your throat

is this how poems start?

when insomnia pounds
like spooked black horses

when the day breaks
like car crash glass

tell me, Mickey,
you knew

tell me

does a poem start
with a hook in the throat?

Dreaming young blondes

Was it the curry?

Bev and Michelle's dinner party
great grog, shit food

bloody vegetarians

those half raw beans playing
in my plumbing for hours

and after a gallon of mint tea
those hot strange dreams

three young blondes
Jodie Foster, Mickey and me

but I'm not young or blonde!

then Jodie fades

Mickey's grip tightens on my arm

she's smiling
at a face I can't see

her arm clutching mine
is all bone
her hair flies
like seaweed

she's whispering
into my mouth

her breath's rotten

but her breasts
against my resisting arm
are sweet

I stop struggling

Mickey, you heard me,
I said yes

yes, yes, yes

I said yes.

Driving

Along the F1 Freeway
  my car drives itself

I imagine I'm Mickey
  seeing someone

I imagine I'm Mickey
  obsessing, obsessing
    and writing poems.

He's married
he led me on
he's scared

what's he frightened of?

he told me he loved me
why are his big hot hands
    around my throat?

oh Mickey, Mickey, Mickey

thank God, I'm a dyke
thank God, I'm not romantic.

Consent

Were you raped Mickey?

Or did you go along
with it

doing what he wanted
because he might be nice

afterwards?

And he wasn't nice
when it hurt

he wasn't nice
when you tried to push him off

he wasn't nice
when you couldn't breathe.

And you weren't there
when he finally came

you weren't there
to say I forgive you

you weren't there
to touch your bruises

you weren't there
to want to go home

you weren't there
to be nice to

afterwards.

The witty couple

'They're such a witty couple'

the woman's breath
    smells of chewing gum

oh christ, an ex-smoker

'Nick and Diana?'
  I say stupidly

the woman
  bumps the plate
    of garlic rolls

one drops in my lap

'Sorry'
  she giggles
    rubbing at the buttery smudge
      on the crotch of my levis

I edge away
  and watch Nick
  pouring Diana
a glass of red
  so red

it looks like menstrual blood

he says something
she says something back

the table cracks up

'They're such a witty couple'
    I remind
      my dinner companion

her drunk eyes
    flicker over
my pack of Benson and Hedges.

Nothing

The patter of rain
the pull of my pants
  around my ankles

her face between my legs

her tongue stops

'What do you think of
when I suck you?'

I catch my breath
  and lie
'Your mouth.'

her tongue starts
and an old mental porn flick
sparks

I come
clutching her hair in fists

'What do you think of
when Nick sucks you?'

she licks a circle
on my inner thigh

'Nothing.'

Money for nothing

'Lou, I feel like I'm talking
to a bunch of accountants

they keep asking
is there much money
in my line of work

I'm learning a lot
from these poets –
computers and tax evasion.'

'It's a grabby, grotty world
not much to go around.
Blame patronage, Jill,
grants, fellowships,
Writers-in-Residence
all that crap . . .

the kids go in
bright-eyed and bushy-tailed
the girls think they're Plath
without the loony bin
the boys wanna be discontinuous heroes
like a good-on-ya mate version
of Carver or Ondaatje

then the little buggers
have to watch
the smart old frauds
and smart young crawlers
split the spoils

and where's the poem in this?
they ask the dole
the dirty flat
and the genital warts

their zingy lives
blow out

while the deadshits
with the contacts
and gift of post-modernist gab
grab what's going.'

'What about you, Lou?'

'I've done the seventies trip, Jill,
I lived with an ideologically
small publisher
who couldn't flog a book
to her own mother

the pub readings
where you were lucky
to get a free beer

I reckon it's my turn
money for nothing
and my chicks for free.'

Chilli breath

'Marcus Woddle strikes again!'
Louie
  stabs her vegie roll

'Who?'
  my voice faint under my hangover
I light up a smoke
  and tell my eyes
    to listen

while the rest of me
  floats back to Diana

'A stooge of Bill McDonald's
on the Writers' Committee'

friends
  stooges or otherwise
    of Bill McDonald's
      are my business

but all I can hear
  is Diana's voice
    tickling

'That bastard Marcus
knocked me back for a grant,
that makes three times in a row!'

'Oh . . . not again, Lou'
  my hand
    dreamy
      on the sugar bowl

'Stop thinking about that fucking woman!'

'Marcus W . . . Woddle'
  I stutter on the stupid name
'can't sit on the committee forever'

'No'
  Lou whispers
    her red chilli breath in my face

'but Bill McDonald can
  in one form or fucking other.'

she grabs her fork

I push back my chair

these poets are hot haters.

A lapse

'Poor Jill'

Louie says
  stroking my hair

my head in her lap

I like the tremble
  in her voice

I close my eyes

and push back
  into her big breasts

her finger
  traces my cheekbone
'you're beautiful'

her breast heaves
  under my ear

she leans over

and kisses me

typical Lou
  not waiting for a second chance

her tongue jumps
  into my mouth

dozily I lick her lip

she doesn't taste right

she doesn't taste like

that heaven
  coffee lipstick cigarettes

I sit up

'Louie, you're my best friend.'

Rear view mirror

In the dark rear view
mirror

my face looks too young

in the dark rear view
mirror

is it Mickey?

in the dark rear view
mirror

my eyes look stoned

headlights

headlights
that make me forget

my face

headlights
that won't go away.

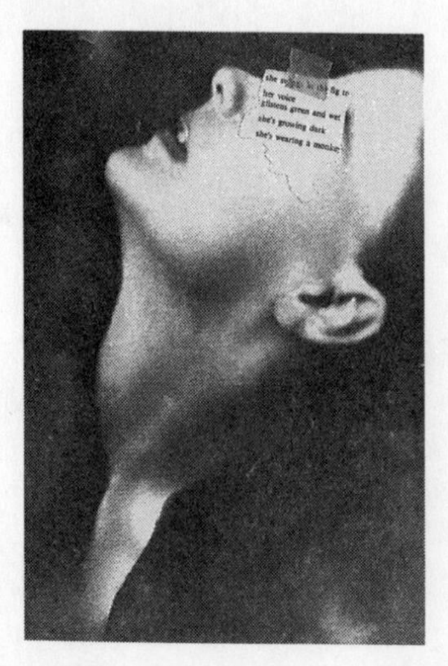

VERSE AND JESUS

Selected Verse

A cup of coffee
a full pack of smokes

and my feet up

bribes
before I could face
Bill's *Selected Verse*

not even a double scotch
could get me through
this fucking poem

in twenty-three parts

finding God in a paddock
when Bill was full
of doubts and pimples

oh, mate,
we should swap
spiritual experiences

I'll never forget the day
I was full of the hots
and Diana's pink nipples.

Steve

Steve's face is always smooth

no matter how late
in the afternoon
he smells of Old Spice

he relaxes with me

elbow to elbow
at the bar
we smoke, down middies
and wish buckets of shit
on bent cops

Steve's straight
struggling on a Homicide Squad
salary

when we're pissed
we plan armed hold-ups
and contract killings

we tell each other
we'd both have big views
of the Harbour
if we weren't mugs
if we weren't honest

this afternoon we're sober

Steve keeps stubbing out
half-smoked fags

he goes through a packet
in an hour

his throat rattles

'Jill' he says

'you've got to leave
this one alone.

There's been a complaint.
You're harassing a certain party.
You're giving us hassles.

Tell Mickey's parents
you've done all you can.

Off the record, Jill,
take what's left of your fee
and run.'

'Bill McDonald.'
I say.

Steve rubs his soft chin.

'It's a woman.'

My teeth hit my glass.

'That's all, mate,'
he says

'just drop it.'

Got him

I went through a bottle
of first class white
reading Mickey's poems

hundreds of them
in different inks
bad handwriting

I read them all

someone had ground her
in the dirt

her killer?

or were the poems
part of the fun?

tear me up
hurt me stuff

no
that's my scene
not Mickey's

she was young
in love
on the line

who isn't at nineteen?

Is Lou right?
was there more than one
beautiful man?

hard to imagine
taking the bastards
that seriously

but it was all there

the rush in the blood
the kick in the guts.

and something else

sweaty, nasty
like a missionary
with a prayer book
in one hand
and a damp erection
in the other

Bill McDonald.

The bait

'Bill?'

'Speaking.'

under the ponce phone voice
he's nervous

he's been waiting for me

'It's Jill Fitzpatrick.'

'Who?'

'We've met, Bill'.

he clears his throat
'What do you want?'

'Just a chat
about some poems.'

'My poems?'

give me a modest novelist!

'No, mate, not this time.
Mickey's poems.

She'll never be on the H.S.C.
unless posthumously,
but her work has a nice turn
of phrase
a bit like yours.'

'I'm hanging up.'

'I'm visiting a pal
at the *Herald*
these poems deserve a big audience.'

'They've got nothing to do with me.'

'Have you read them all, Bill?'

I rustle some paper
and smack my lips

'They're not what my Mum
would call discreet.'

the phone hums
as we make a date.

Centennial Park

Hot and dark
no moon

I can't see him

his voice close
and dangerous

I can smell him

let him talk
let him brag

he must be busting

crackle of twigs
the stifling air shifts

he's coming closer

something shines
he's got a knife

my gun's in the car

'Jesus
wouldn't like this'

a smart arse feint

'He came with a sword'
the maniac hisses

'to cut up vermin like you.'

A quote
I need Jesus on my side

'What about Love Your Enemy?'

'The Devil quotes Scripture
for his own purpose

you lesbian filth!'

the knife gleams
the knife trembles

his hand's not steady

neither's my nerve
my gut griping

will he go for my face?

keep talking
push him over the edge

he'll make a mistake

'Mickey. Mickey.'
I chant like a game

'Tell Uncle Jesus about Mickey

tell your big clean Christ
what you did to Mickey

show Mister God your dirty dick!'

I've done it
he's gibbering

he's gushing

abuse, the Bible
all the spill

of a canting gutter

but my bones know
he's not forgotten

his pure weapon, his knife

get him
while he's ranting

hit him now.

Fear me

at my crust
I'm violent

right down deep
I'm violent

at my finger tips
I'm violent

in the glands of my breasts
I'm violent

in the shield of my cervix
I'm violent

in my feral womb
I'm violent

fear me fear me fear me

I'm female.

Fight

The dark jumps
like a funnel-web

Bill's hand
which hand?

brushes my shoulder
softly

where's the knife?
I dodge under his breath

kick
my leg's listening

straight
into his invisible crotch

got him

get him down
he's twice my size

not enjoying this
he's snivelling

'Stop it!'

his hand boneless

'Please
I threw it away'

where is it?

my foot gets clever
tips the blade

I've had him

cut his whining throat

'Mickey'
he whimpers

still bent double
cuddling his balls

'I loved her
loved her'

'With this?'
I flick the knife at his hair

'It wasn't me!'

I can smell his tears
hot like snot

'Mickey'
he blubs

I believe him.

Heavy breathing

Bill follows me
to my car

I open the door
curse my mechanic

who never fixed
the inside light

dark night
dark car

Bill stands close
still blubbering

'Mate,' I say
'it's been a long night.'

and clench my keys
in my trembling fist

'Sorry' he touches my arm
'Sorry' he chokes

I pat his shoulder
and pray my car starts

'The phone calls'
he whispers

'those phone calls'
his chest heaves

Key in the ignition.
Dash lights up.

'What phone calls, Bill?'
engine turns over

'Why couldn't you leave
Mickey and me alone?'

My heavy breather.
My poet of dirty threats.

I pump the pedal

'Stick that poem you left
on my answering machine

in your *Collected*.
It's one of your best.'

and I take off.

The power of Them

'I'm finished I'm finished'

Bill whimpering on the phone

'it's all gone wrong gone wrong'

I let him talk
no knife between us now

'she broke me she broke me first'

I let him talk
what can he give me?

'I spat on the Holy Spirit.
She made me write filth.'

do I need a critic
or an exorcist?

'I'll show you show you tomorrow'

Not more bloody poems!

'what she made me write
what she showed them'

'Showed what
to who, Bill?'

'I gave her up gave her up
couldn't trust her'

he's raving

'they got her.
she went to them.'

'Who?'
  my arms prickling

'evil they made me evil'
he's off again

he'll spill

I murmur like a priest
make a time

and hear his hiss
as he hangs up.

Spilling the beans

Why is Diana's phone
  always engaged?

Come on. Come on.

Finally.

'Who you been yakking to?

Have I got news!

A long story.
Bill's cracked.

He's coming here.

Why the big drive?

Mountain air, baby,
good for the soul
good for spilling the beans.'

Waiting for Bill

I've always hated
Sunday afternoons.

The mist's coming in.
I don't have a video.

Blue Hawaii on TV.
I can't hack Elvis.

My car's stuffed.

And Patsy just gets me
drinking.

What's Diana doing?
Friends in for drinkies?
Backyard barbie?
Clever chat over a short black
in Oxford Street?

As long as she's dressed.

Someone's dog is barking.
It sounds chained up.

Dying slow

Steve sneaked me
the police report

I owe him a big drink.

The car went off
like a bomb

Bill was trapped.

The fuel line leaking
so was the brake fluid

Bill had Buckley's.

Driving like a mad bastard
down the Hawkesbury Road

just a matter of time.

The Mountains are so used
to horrors

ghosts shiver in the bush.

But this must have shaken
the tired old crumbles

out of all that haunted sandstone.

Bill died slow
Bill's hands stuck

like liquorice to the windows.

Not even a bad poet
not even a born-again hypocrite

deserves to burn at the stake

of his own car.

Flirting with the cops

Steve buys me a cider
  at the Glebe Rowers

'I only wanted a Lite'
I say
  and swallow an apple brew
    with the kick of a mule

'I want some information'
  he grins

'And I thought you wanted my body.'

why is he the only man
  I flirt with?

Steve gives me a foxy smile
and rubs his perfumed cheeks

'What was Bill McDonald doing
on the Hawkesbury Road,
did he have a cuppa
at your place, Jill?'

'Jealous?'

'Curious.
And so's the coroner.'

I stroke the back
of his soft hand

Steve looks me in the face
he's moderately married

'Don't start something
you can't stop'

he smiles
he can be cute too

then his hand flips and grips

'Don't fuck me around.
Did you see Bill
that afternoon?'

'No!'

he lets me go

'Keep the rough stuff
for your wife'
I flap my smarting hand
in his face

he catches and kisses it
'Did Bill have a special poem
just for you?'

'He lost his nerve
if he did'

Steve tries to stare me out
'How do you know?'

'You'll never make sergeant, Steve.
He was driving down the mountain
not up to my place.'

'What turned him around?'

our hands lying close
on the bar

I touch his hairy wrist
with my pinkie

'God.'

Mystery

Who killed Mickey?
Who fiddled with Bill's car?

I don't have clues.

No evidence
just a smell
of sex and violence.

And pages of Mickey's words.

Diana tells me
words are erotic
yet really mean bugger all.

'you're my beautiful secret'

Mickey was meaning
someone.

It's not all
a mystery to me.

Every breath she takes

She's not with me

she comes too quickly
    rolls on her back
    crosses her arms
      over her breasts
and stares at the ceiling

'Is anything wrong?'

I hate the whimper
    in my voice

'No'
  she says
her face
  so shut off
I watch
  the rise and fall
    of her chest.

Strange fun

Over coffee
it's no better
she stares at a spot
over my shoulder
and won't talk

'Bill told me
something strange
the day before he died'

I try
with the old bait
of the Mickey case

her eyes fix on me
'What did he say?'

I grin
gratefully

'Well, darling'
I gurgle
'you might be able
to help me here
he wasn't making much sense'

'What did he say?'

her eyes bright
her face white

my lips start prickling

she smiles
taking my hand

her palm is sweaty

'C'mon, baby, spit it out
what was on Jesus-Loves-Me's mind?'

I stroke her thumb

what's the matter?
what's the matter with her?

I talk slowly

'He was all over the place.
    Frightened. Upset.
He was going to show me
  some poems'

I stroke her knuckles

'evil poems.'

Diana laughs

'Let me guess—
constipated verses
  to poor little Mickey
about their secret, sordid
  sex life.'

'Probably'
  I pause and watch her

'but someone else
got hold of them'

she pulls her hand away

'Satan?
We must track them down, sweetie.'

I won't play

'Someone'
  I say
    as if to myself
'was having a lot of fun
      with Bill.'

Mrs Bill McDonald

I don't bother phoning
I wait

  and catch her at home

'Mrs McDonald?
  Sorry to disturb you.'

she's small, my age,
  daggy neat clothes
    that unmistakable fashion label
      'Born-Again Christian'

her eyes are pale
    and mournful

I flash some ID
  and mumble
'I'm working with the police'

she buys it
  and lets me in

'Tragic business.
Your husband was a fine poet.'

she nods mutely
her eyes watery

'Is this a bad time?'

her voice comes
  as a surprise
loud
  much tougher
    than her eyes

'When will the coroner
    be finished
      with Bill's body?'

I swallow back bullshit
and tell the truth

'I don't know.
Ring in a few days.
Hassle.
You've got rights, love.'

she stares
I don't sound like a cop

'I need to go through
Bill's papers.'

she shrugs
and turns away
to blow her nose

'Come this way'
 she says muffled
  in a lace hanky.

Guard wife

Bill's computer
  sits precious
    under its cover

pens in one cup
pencils in another

books to the ceiling
I wave at them

'Did he get around
  to reading all these?'

his wife picks out
a book of Bill's poems
with a cover
  of blue poofy orchids

she turns to a special page
  and ignores me

'I want to see the poems
  he was working on.'

she looks up

'Why?'

'It's important'
  I pause
'to know his state of mind
  before he died.'

she's trembling

'You're not suggesting
    he killed himself?'

'We can't rule that out.'

I'm all ice
 as she pulls out
  a folder

it's empty

she folds her arms
  over her nothing breasts

and smiles

'Where are they?'
I want to shake her

'Gone'
  she whispers

'gone
  where no-one will find them.'

I leave her
    hugging herself
      in Bill's study.

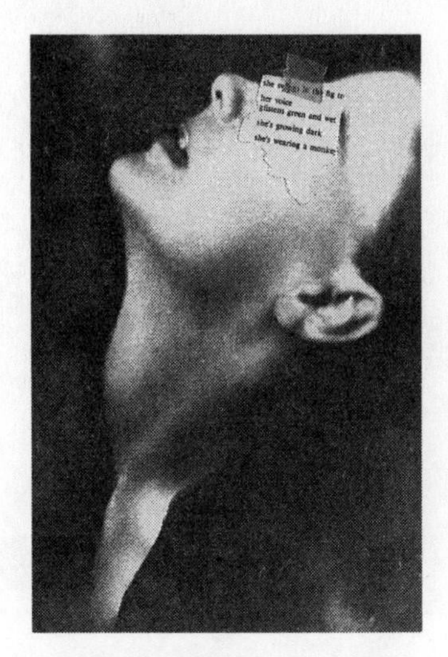

BRISBANE

One down

Mickey's pin-up poets.

One down.
One to go.

Bill's gone.
That leaves Tony.

But how could he
have sabotaged Bill's car
from Brisbane?

And did he screw Mickey?

Barbara's wobbly.

Wound in paranoia
like wire
around sticks of gelli
she's unstable
    and bloody dangerous.

Did Tony run to Brisbane
before Barbara
    could go off in his face?

Did Tony rape and strangle
  his pretty little fan?

Is Tony running from a wife
      or a ghost?

If she rings

she said
she'd ring in a week

two weeks ago

we were walking along
Balmoral Beach

we were almost
holding hands

we were watching
seagulls

our salty lips
her nervy hand
skipping chips
through the sand

she said
she was marking essays
she said
she'd ring in a week

two weeks ago

this morning
I'm not waiting by the phone

this morning
I'm packing my bags

if she rings in an hour
I'll be on the train

if she rings later
I'll be on the plane

if she rings tonight
I'll be in Brisbane

at least a hundred beaches
away.

Tony's charm

Tony is charming
and comfortable

his poems are depressed
like sleeping pills

I got to page three
of his *Selected*

but Tony's generous
with his time

he talks about Mickey
with laid-back affection

'A nice kid'
he says

'her poetry was awful
but she was a nice kid'

we light up
in chummy silence

'a really nice kid'
he sucks down
   a deep drag

'I haven't seen her for months'

his hands lie still
and bland

'not for months.'

Tony's company

Tony's voice
is a lullaby Mogadon

but he likes a joke

we snigger through
my time
in the poetry scene

but even
with the passionfruit smell
of a Brisbane night

Tony's company
is hard cold work

like defrosting a fridge.

Frangipani

I thought poets
were broke

Tony's house
is high and airy

the breeze carries
frangipani from the garden

from his long verandah
he can watch the Brisbane River

does he sit sipping his tea
in some fragrant twilight

and write
his miserable poetry?

Mickey Monkey

'To Brisbane'
    Tony toasts the scented dark
    'The City of Snooze'

I'm going under
    the soft warm night's
        anaesthetic

Tony's next toast
    kicks me awake

'To Mickey'
    and he stops

'To Mickey'
    he repeats
        and slurps from his glass

'Once upon a time –
        Mickey the Monkey
        all knowing cunning
            little hands
        she knew where the nuts
            were hidden
        and, jesus, she knew
            how to squeeze –'

he stares into his drink
    and tips it
        over the back of his hand

I gasp

he licks it off
there was only
        a trickle

'A solemn libation'
    he says
'to whom we're blessed with
    now

Mickey the Martyr.'

Truth and Beauty

'Young women
   have their drawbacks'

Tony crosses his legs
   flashing a lairy pair
      of socks

'Mickey had to write
every fucking thing down'

I'm drinking too much red
   I nod to keep him talking

'filled books with her fucking poems'
he laughs
'fucking poems, all right

she didn't give a shit
   about Truth and Beauty
      just fucking'

he's downed a six pack
   his working-class origins
      raring to go

'she even kept a bloody diary,
   like most budding poetesses
she couldn't leave her love life alone.'

I swallow the smoothest
   mouthful of red
      I've ever had

'Where's her diary now?'
   I sound too keen

Tony pats his small pot belly
   and eyes me slowly off

'Not with me, baby.

Ask Diana.
   It gave her a good laugh.

An embarrassment of riches.'

Lotsa laughs

Seeing me out
Tony pauses at the door

a paw
on my shoulder
to steady himself

he treats me
to a thoughtful sigh
of beery breath

'Waddya make
of the lovely Doctor Di?'

smacking his lips

'Octane fuel, octane mind?'

a watery wink

'I guess you two
have lotsa laughs

just don't let her
have the last one, love.'

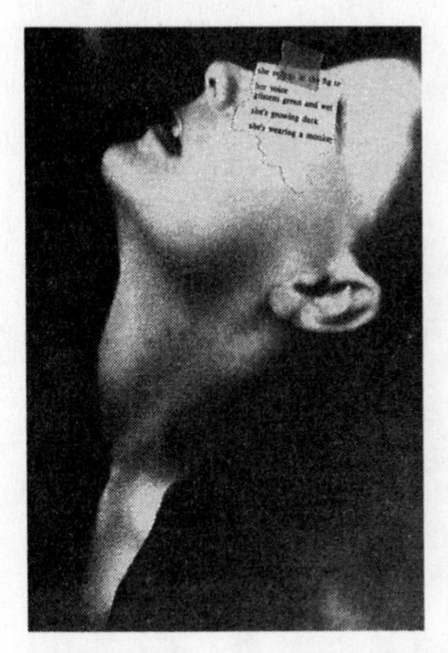

THE EMPTY UNIVERSITY

Ignoring the evidence

Flying over the red roofs
and blinding water
of my glittering tart Sydney

I know Diana's a liar

the plane's wheels bump down
hard

and I know I'm a fool

Mickey's diary will name
names

Mickey's diary will point the finger
at me

for ignoring the evidence.

I put a spell on you

A parrot shrieks
over my ivy-smothered letterbox

I shake off the snails
  gnawing the edges
    of bills, junk and an envelope
      in a strange hand
addressed 'Jill, The Detective'

a smart arse

I open it first

and out falls
    a poem in laser print
    on pink paper

I put a spell on you, my beautiful man,
I put LSD in your short black
so you can see me in wild colours
with rats spinning round my bruised face
you know what you did, I know too
so I put a spell on you
you can't kill or bury me
because I'll name you wherever you are
my lover, my lover, my man, my big fist,
I know pain but I know magic better.

Another Mickey poem.

Who sent it?
Someone with a crash-hot printer.

Someone determined I know
  how the beautiful man
    likes his coffee.

Stand by your poet

The phone.

No rush.

It won't be Diana.

'How's Tony?'
    a flat female voice

'Who's asking?'

'His wife.'

'Barbara?'

'How many wives
    do you think he has?
He's not a fucking Mormon!'

not the time
  to spar with Barb

I let her hang herself
  in my dead silence

'Are you still there?'

she bangs the phone

'Jill? Jill?'

this is fun

a low sobbing sigh

'Barbara . . .'
  I let her off the hook
'he didn't kill that girl.'

what's she doing?
does she believe me?

a suck of breath
    until she gets
        her old old bearings

'My husband
     shouldn't be disturbed

my husband
     went to Brisbane

to write.'

Dear Jill

Squinting
I drive through the mist

the phone goes

'Who?'
Crackle. Crackle.

'Diana?'
I'm smiling.

'What?'

I turn a bend
I can hear her

the mist clears

median strip, milk bars
mouse-hole houses

grey, everything's grey

she's breaking it off
long distance

she doesn't even say
Dear Jill.

The empty university

Is this work or revenge?

It's semester break
and the place is quiet.

I know she's away.

My fingers look forward
to breaking in.

The empty lift

The lift tinkles 'California Dreaming'

in a stale reek
of cigarettes and B.O.

standing in this empty lift
is like standing
    in a dirty mouth.

Her office

Diana's desk

Diana's chair

Diana's lip-sticked
  coffee cup

and a litter of memos
my eyes scrummage
    for her scribbly gum
      handwriting

that's not what I broke in for

I'm a burglar
can't sit around
all afternoon
  in a fool's fug
    of her things

right.
Mickey's diary.

a locked top drawer
time for my bracelet of keys

probe, fiddle, click

tampons, money, business letters
and a packet of photos.

Nick. They're all of Nick.

Except this one.

Nick's got company.
Diana and Mickey.

Her smell

The stairwell

the hand set
of the blue phone

even the jerking lift

are all terrible
with her smell

as if her hair
is spilling into my nose

every silent minute.

Mickey's diary

It's gone, Mickey.

I'll have to go on your poems
and guesswork.

I wish I'd got to it
before she did.

She didn't spare it.
She didn't spare you.

But thank God
she spared

her precious boy's photo.

Chasing my tail

Five Cars Back
the classic tail

she shoots the lights
don't lose her

shit
Volvo hogging fast lane

her car
the blur of her head

a sharp left
stick with her

turn off
the blah blah blah radio

heart fast
nerves sharp

nothing like
follow that blonde!

nothing like
the exhaust fumes

of your own deceitful lover.

What a knife can do

It's the dope
it's not really me

I've smelled blood
I've seen what a knife can do

why am I seeing Diana
dead?

her throat slit
her blood

sick
my mind should be shot

I've seen what a knife can do.

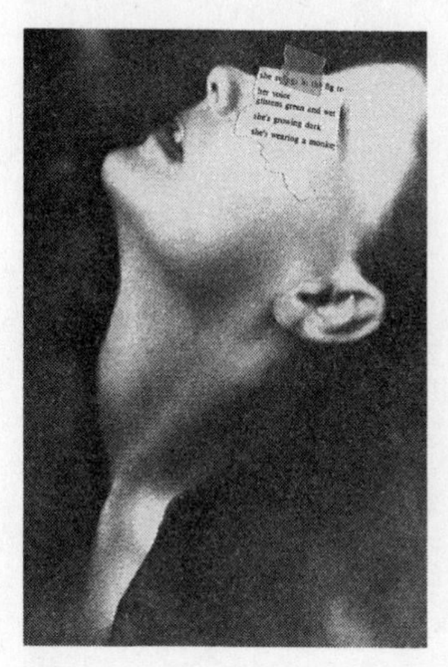

THE WANING MOON

Not cricket

Red bottlebrush
on railway stations

wet kids
flapping around pools

summer's coming

swimming, drinking
parties and cricket.

I've got work to do.

It can't just be Diana.
They're all linked up.

Tony's talked
but Barbara's angry

she might talk more

poke the tiger snake
let it strike

then milk it dry.

Barbara's venom

Barbara is wrinkled
but petitely pretty

in the unflattering sun

she doesn't like me
but it's not personal

she doesn't like PIs

I wonder
if she got pissed off

having Tony watched

years and years
of reports and dirty photographs

don't endear a profession

but she's not too proud
to stuff her face

on my expense account

she knows I know
about Tony and Mickey

does she still care?

she threw him out
she's winning

she's got a flash new job

her cautious eyes
her small neat teeth

chew on me

like she's got
a hot ace

to flutter on the table

her smile
dull gold metal

'Diana told Tony everything

she told him
you made a pass

a big pass at her.'

my silence is confirmation
my trembling mouth

is pitiful

my lovely post-modernist Marxist
so good at rewriting

history

'That's not the whole story'
I say

rallying a little

'Don't waste your time'
Barbara pulls the pin

'she's been seeing Tony

off and on
for months

she's nuts about him.'

Sleeping around

I find Lou
submerged
in the dyke section
at Gleebooks

'Jill!'
she jumps
slipping *Lesbian Erotica*
back on the shelf

'You look terrible.
What's happened?'

'Diana's fucking Tony.'

'That all?'
smacking my shoulder
'I thought someone else
had got bumped off.'

'Barbara told me.'

'That's one crazy woman.
You're mad
if you listen to her.'

outside
Glebe Point Road
flows
with chic skinny
kids

I remember Mickey
and the fun she's missing

Lou takes my arm

'Why are you so amazed
your goddess
sleeps around?'

'I was hoping
she had better taste.'

'Oh, she has, she has.
She married
Golden Boy, Quick Nick,
champion of the crippled crim
scourge of the fascist courts . . .

but she likes to play
she likes to take
a holiday.'

Poisons

I used to think nicotine
was my poison

I still smoke two packs
on a moderate day

cigarettes are not my poison

I used to think poetry
was Mickey's poison

she wrote a hundred and thirty-two poems
in three months

poetry didn't poison Mickey

I used to think religion
was Bill's poison

everything he wrote
was a bribe to Jesus

religion didn't kill Bill

I wanted my body
to be Diana's poison

I wanted someone to pass her
the bottle

love, love,
   oh poisonous love.

She once asked

Shaving my legs
in a lukewarm bath

my hand is her hand
as it runs down my soapy calf

'Have you ever tried a threesome?'
she once asked

'No' I said

fantasising
her on one side

and a blonde on top
her silky hair in my mouth

someone like Mickey

'Not another woman'
she said

'a man.'

Fishy

Diana's in the bath with me

slippery between my legs

her scales
gleam black and gold

inside me she swims
a cold finger

I can't come

the water's
over my head

watch this
says a fish

it's Nick

his gold scales stink

he dives into
Mickey's green head

he swims out
of one of her eyes

catch ya later catch ya later
he winks

wake up

I reach across my wet pillow
for my smokes.

Bluff

I watch her peel
a mango

I watch her play
with the buttons on her shirt

I watch her fiddle
with her wine glass

we aren't talking much

until I say
'I know about Mickey's diary.'

'I hope' Diana says
'it makes better reading than her poetry.'

I raise her
'It wasn't bad enough to burn.'

she won't blink

'I imagine most of it
was wishful thinking

like her poetry.'

I drink my coffee too fast
it isn't brandy

and burn my tongue

'Did she meet Nick
through you?'

Diana concentrates
on the sugar bowl

'You and Barbara Knight
make very strange bedfellows

she tells her shrink
fairy stories too

she'll leave you
with egg on your face.'

Christ, is Diana spilling!
I'll get back to Barbara.

Now for lay-down *misère.*

'The diary had a lot
of wishful thinking

a lot of fairy stories too
about Nick.'

Diana's eyes glitter

'Did dear little Barbara
tell you
I'm fucking Tony?'

I nod
and wink across the table
'All the way from Brisbane?

Wow.
He must have the longest dick
in Australia.'

Anal attitude

Diana looks at the label
on my instant coffee

'You've got an anal attitude
to money.'

The waning moon

The sky is hot
  Turkish blue
the half moon
  glows white

we lie on our backs
  in the curve
    of a cool sandstone rock

and talk

'What do you see in Tony?'
  I ask off-hand

'Lots of things'
    her answer is light
      cool

'he's a brilliant man.'

brilliant?
those bored eyes?

'This sky is brilliant'
  I point
    with a shaky hand

'not him.'

Diana sits up

'You sound like
  one of Mickey's poems.'

everything
  shuts off

she drives back
  to the city.

AZT and Sympathy

Late,
oh, fuck, I'm drunk
late
   I ring Louie

'She's worthless'

I'm raving

'Worthless?'
   Louie pauses
      to swallow

she's always eating

'Worth
   is a patriarchal construct
not to mention
   capitalistic
verging on the Kerry Packer, Jill.'

'She's a virus'

I'm off

'she's an opportunistic infection
she's a tongue load of thrush
she's needles and shingles
she's the kiss of herpes
she's a wasting flu'

'Sounds like Kali'
   Louie musing and munching

'I'm H-Diana-V-Positive!'

'Waddya want?
A.Z.T. and Sympathy?'

'She's separating my meat
from my bones'

I'm drum rolling
I'm pathetic

'she's gone, Lou.'

I get to the point.

Ghost poet

Barbara lights up
  but shuts the packet shut
before I can bludge

her pretty eyes squint
  in her smoke

'A dead girl sent me
  a poem, Barb.'

I twirl her classy lighter
  in a pool of stale beer

she snatches it

'A poem from heaven.
Did God let Mickey use
  His best laser printer?'

'What the fuck are you talking about?'

'I put a spell on you'
I sing loudly

'Shut up!'
  chewing off her lipstick

'I was a smart girl, Barb,
I followed all the clues

goodness me, Tony drinks tea
while Nick likes his coffee . . .'

Barbara grinds out her fag.

'Tell Tony from me
he writes his best poems
when he's ghosting for Mickey.'

Barbara looks at me

and flips the ash-tray
  into my lap.

Wives and root rats

Barbara and Diana
have something in common
besides hating each other

they're loyal wives

Mrs Bill McDonald
ran in the same maze

you love the bastard
you cover his shit.

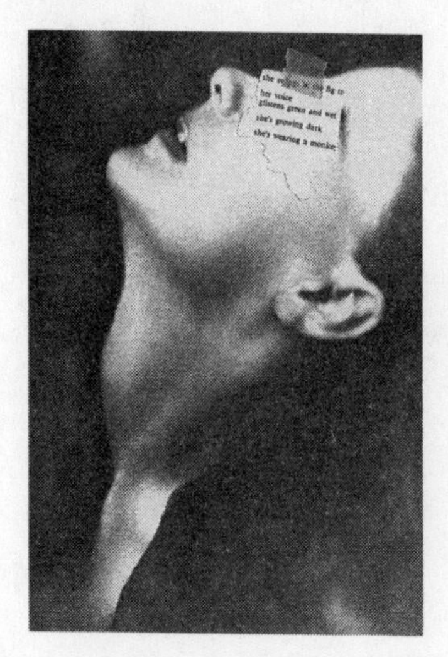

IT AIN'T NECESSARILY SO

Luck

Useless to bother
fortune tellers, the stars
or Runes

luck leaps on the floor
like a glob of mercury

one night
it deserted Mickey

it wasn't even gleaming
in a crack.

Today
what's this grimy shine
under my finger nails?

Luck's slimy trail?

Barbara's visit

I see her
before she sees me

sitting in her Saab
in a fug of smoke

my car bumps and rattles
into my old garage

I take my time
getting out

we meet with big smiles
at my crooked front gate

I sweep my arm
towards my flowering weeds

'Have you come
to admire my rhododendrons?'

Barbara's red nails
bite the gate

'I've come a long way.
Can I have some coffee?'

'Welcome to my favourite café.
My cat makes a great short black.'

She raises her eyebrows
and follows me silently

I take a drag of sweet cold air
and wonder what she wants

she watches me
spooning out the instant

'I know who killed Bill'
she caresses the words

'Stale news, Barb,' I say
over the rumble of the boiling jug.

Oil and grease

Emma squirms
in a white warm ball
at Barbara's feet

'Could you put it outside'
she sniffs
'I'm allergic to cats.'

I leave my moggy
stretching an arching paw
towards Barbara's panty-hosed ankle

and light a cigarette

Barbara shows her teeth
her eyes
little blue holes

and clears her throat

'Your lover might fix
your car one day
like she fixed Bill's.'

I consider this

'Well, she couldn't do
a worse job
than my local mechanic

does she throw in an oil and grease?'

Barbara gets up slowly

'You're not funny.
You're just way out
of your fucking depth.'

I take her to the door

'Lovely to see you.
Do I owe the pleasure
to Tony

or jealousy?'

Cold

I wait for Barbara
to have the last word
put the boot in
kick over a chair

she's usually good value

instead
she goes to my smudged window
and stares at the clouds
blowing over in a quick wind

'I don't know
how you stand it'
she whispers

'Stand what?'

'The cold. The fucking cold.'

Flashes

I've got a fish pond

for me
not the fish

it settles the mind

my kind of meditation

as my mung mix
of brown and gold fish
flash underwater

my mind flashes too

flash of gold filmy tail
flash of floating hair

it's time to see Nick.

Leave it

Why did she do it?

leave it
till morning

not now
   in the dark

with your skin crawling

oh, you were ready
   you were eager
wet and open
   as Sydney Harbour

what cunt wouldn't she suck
   to get Nick off the hook?

you were her party chook
   headless

smell no evil
hear no blood.

Dinner for two

Nick has a white smile
and a striped shirt

he tells lawyer jokes
while we wait for the soup

his fingers tap the glass
of the ash tray

I see his fingers
cupping Diana's breast

he's flirting with me
nervously

he smells as sweet
as a woman

he touches my wrist
with a flick of his hand

'You should grow your hair.'

I've lost my appetite

I hear Diana telling him
'Dykes always go for me.'

Nick lets out his hair

Nick lets out his hair

it fans
blonde, silky

he could be a pin-up
he could be a girl

his sweet smell
is suffocating

I let down a window

he eases his bum
on the car seat

and stretches his legs

'You've done wonders
for my wife'

his caressing nerve

'her eyes shine
after she's fucked you
what were you girls drinking, hey?'

his hair glimmering
across a smooth cheek

bones too big
for a pretty woman's face

can't get a handle
on this effeminate man

like a transvestite
in a tiger skin mini
making a dark alley pass

his soft hand curls like a rip
around my breast

my nipple helplessly swims
in his palm

he's not a girl
he's not a girl

my nipple's
not listening

my hand fists
to hit him

fear curdling
in my mouth

tastes like dream lust

where you're not yourself
where you don't care
where you could fuck a goat

'Let me go
or I'll break your arm'

my voice is full of water

he's not a girl
he's not a girl

I stare at his crotch

'Touch me'

his voice
sea-weed dragging down
my legs

my hand

drops then stops

he's unzipped
a thick pink prick

he's not a girl

'suck me'

his voice like stubble

'make my eyes shine too!'

eyes, eyes
like *bullets and knives*

Mickey's demon lover

'You killed Mickey.'

he laughs
like a man
like a cold shower

and pushes my hand down

I go with it
then close my fingers
around him

I'm throttling a snake

his eyes bulge
his hands flail
to punch my face

my free hand chops him
in the throat

his dick dies
in my hand

I let him go

'Put it away
or I'll feed it
to my cat.'

he's catching his breath
his arms knot like stones

he'll grind me to bits

it's my car
I can't run

'Catch ya later'

he's out of the car

he's smiling
he waves me off

like he had fun
like he won.

Like her

My breath

my pants still sticky

in the tree
something black

squeaking

I could have ended up
like Mickey

giving in
going with it

his hair. his smell.

I don't even like boys

didn't stop me
nearly ending up

like her.

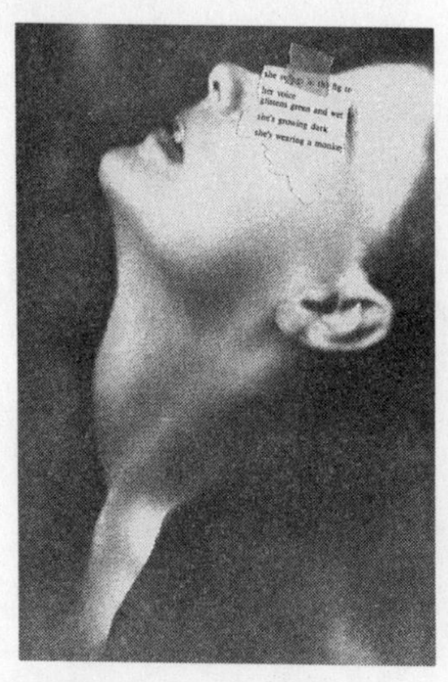

THE MONKEY'S MASK

Reckless, careless and sexy

So good to be home
so good to be alone

so good to spin out
a pot of tea

I'm here
Mickey isn't

did she die
so Nick wouldn't die
of boredom?

or his clever clever wife?

both of them
reckless, careless
  and sexy
both of them
  running on empty

but the cops
will never know

reckless, careless
  sex killed Mickey

I know
because

reckless, careless sex
  nearly killed me.

Heading north

Heading north over the Bridge

the wind is warm
and smells of petrol

if I light a match
I might go up

rehearsing my wrap-up
to Mickey's parents

'She wasn't murdered
it was an accident'

then what?
Freud? Masters and Johnson?

get the experts to explain
this mess

'it was sex play
that went wrong'

Mrs Norris' missionary position
face

gagging on the broken hyoid bone
of her daughter's sex life

while I tell her
strangulation orgasm

is lots safer
between girls?

Oh, the squeeze
of Diana's fingers

shorting me out
like a smoking fuse-box!

Nick takes big risks
with his big hands

I tell them
it's only a hunch

I can't prove
a bloody thing

then change the subject
to money

count the noughts on my cheque
and go?

of course there's always
kind lies and bullshit

do I owe Mickey
more than I owe

my mortgage?

Whose neat scissors?

My cool thoughts of
water, wind and yachts

shift to the shell
of a charred car

shift to Bill McDonald
writing dirty poems

shift to silly Mickey
sharing them with teacher

shift to cruel cats
playing a randy mouse

shift to fear

shift to Bill dropping
his cheese in Nick's claws

shift to Mickey mangled

shift to my lovesick
blabbering mouth

shift to fear

shift to a fire

shift to Bill
soundlessly screaming

whose neat scissors
snipped his fuel line?

whose sophisticated stomach
didn't have to watch?

A big cheque

Their house is so hot
the varnish
on the antique table
bubbles

we sit on the balcony
floating in black air

'I've talked
to all her friends
I've traced
all her movements

I'm sure she wasn't killed
by someone she knew.'

they lean forward
intensely listening
I take half an hour
to tell them nothing

are they peeved
or relieved?

over warm wine
they ask about my work
I dig up the Lebanese family
who keep stealing their own car

insurance fraud jokes
are always racist

both of them laugh
settling
their checks and pleats
in deck chairs

tonight has comfortably
cremated Mickey

at ten o'clock
I get a big cheque
written with a flourish
and a gold fountain pen.

Selling up

A red white and blue
    wooden flag
has been planted
    outside my house

'Bankruptcy!'
  it flaps to the street
'Marital Bust-Up!'
  it flaps like failure

really
  it's a pirate's flag

'New Loot!'
  it flashes

I'm heading
  for the high sea

I'm off
  to Sydney.

The cactus flower

I wake up late this morning
to coffee with Tia Maria
and left-over cheese cake

you don't run sixteen hour days
you don't run with poets

without a big fix of sugar

I count my red eyes

I listen to
the answering machine

Diana's no good with a machine

she can't charm it
stupid

it takes her the full three minutes
after the beep
to say

'Meet you for coffee
Art Gallery three o'clock.'

I'll be there, sweetheart.

More sugar.

And one slow minute
to enjoy the weird flower
on my cactus

it will have shrivelled
to nothing
by the time I get home.

What Diana taught me

She never taught me
   to like real coffee

french novels
obscure boy poets
her terrace renovations

or lies.

She taught me
   to drop my guard

close my eyes
      and fall over.

She taught me
      pleasure.

What girls know
what girls can do.

I owe her.

Steam

Nowhere to park

I chance my luck
and park
down the side of the Gardens

there's a storm
boiling
in the muddy air

my feet
my armpits
steam

I sprint to the Gallery

and get a stitch

gasping
like a teenage boy
after a climax
in the cool polished portals

towards the glass
upstairs
I can see Diana

she's not reading
she's chewing her lip

good

I hit the Ladies
have a wee
splash my face
do my hair

it's still Diana

give me six months
I'll laugh at myself.

Last throw

She orders me a cappuccino
and smiles
running her tongue
that quick pink tip
over her lip

nerves
not a flirt

I still watch her
with a jangled gut

'What are you going to do?'
she says
not wasting time

'What are you going to do?'
I volley.

'Protect my interests.'

no cringing, no crawling

'Don't protect Nick.'
I wipe off
my froth moustache

questions clag in my throat

is it the bastard's money?
what do you owe him?

'You can't make
the mud stick, Jill,
you open your mouth
we'll sue.'

she's smiling
her eyes
show the black pit
of the old woman
she'll become

you can't save her
I slap down my Galahad fool

'Is it his money, sweetheart?
You've sold yourself fucking cheap!'

she's on her feet

my last throw
of lovers' talk

'Mickey's parents'
I say quietly
as she rips through
her bag for her purse

'are mind-bogglingly boring people'

she's still
she's listening

'Nick's really jazzed up their lives –

without Nick
they might never have known
the smell of the morgue

without Nick
they might never have known
the smell
of their daughter's decomposing face.'

oh, Diana, Diana,
my heart palpitates
like a pop song

'Jealousy's making you hallucinate'
she hisses

and she's gone.

The monkey's mask

I walk back to the car
in wild hot rain

rain, rain,
forty days, forty nights

and the inner city drowns

and Diana's terrace floats
out to sea

Forget the bitch.
Case solved.

My hair draggles
in drenched coils
I could be Medusa
out for a stroll

okay, Medusa,
turn all these fuckers
to stone

turn those fraud poets
to marble
a staircase leading nowhere
in a Stalinist museum

turn Nick
to sandstone
and let him crumble

turn Diana . . .
loose.

Mickey's ghost walks
in this tropical rain

she swings in the fig trees

her voice
glistens green and wet

she's growing dark

she's wearing a monkey's mask.